WHAT'S SO FUNNY ABOUT DEPRESSION?

G.G. Maxwell

Copyright © 2024 G.G. Maxwell

All rights reserved

The characters and events portrayed in this book are fictitious. Any similarity to real persons, living or dead, is coincidental and not intended by the author.

No part of this book may be reproduced, or stored in a retrieval system, or transmitted in any form or by any means, electronic, mechanical, photocopying, recording, or otherwise, without express written permission of the publisher.

ISBN: 9798323029242

Cover design by: G.G. Maxwell
Printed in the United States of America

*this book is dedicated to
those with mental illness*

*with special thanks to
my writing coach
Susanne Schotanus*

"Blessed are the meek, for they shall inherit the earth."

MATTHEW 5:5

CONTENTS

Title Page
Copyright
Dedication
Epigraph
SEE JILL RUN — 1
THE BEFORE AND AFTER LIFE — 12
THE MONKEY IN HER PURSE — 24
COME TO CALL — 42
THE MONKEY ON HER BACK — 46
THE DEVIL ON HER SHOULDER — 61
TEN POUND GORILLA — 72
DOWN ON THE FARM — 80
WHAT IS SO FUNNY ABOUT MENOPAUSE? — 92
BLOOD MONEY — 108
EVEN IN CHANEL — 118
SATAN, THE AIR BISCUIT — 119
WINDY CITY WOMAN — 125
PAINTED BLACK — 140
CRICKETS — 151
VON SO-AND-SO — 153
SAGE ON STAGE — 156

DING DONG	165
A VISION IN WHITE	168
QUITE CONTRARY	172
SHOW AND TELL	178
MAD MAX	182
VIVID VOID	183
THE FUTURE WILL BE	185
PICTURE OF YOU	187
DIFFICULT	190
WHERE THE HEART IS	194
I HAVE THE POWER	198
BANG BANG!	199
ON WITH THE SHOW	200
THE HEADLINER	203
WHAT'S SO FUNNY ABOUT DEPRESSION?	205
	209

SEE JILL RUN

The earth was beginning to thaw in who-cares-where, Ohio. In the wee hours of the morning all the lights were on in her mother's house but soon there would be no one home. Jill was seated on the edge of her bed, naked except for her neon running shoes. She was cramming her plus-sized clothes into trash bags, because her heart told her to run and Jill always followed her heart.

She should have gotten dressed before she turned on all the lights in the house that morning because the windows were bare, as Jill never had seen the point in hanging curtains there because she never knew how long she might be staying. Strange logic, considering no one ever really knows how long they will be living anywhere. But Jill no longer had two fucks left to give about that fly over state, or logic, because she was moving on.

She planned to use her A-to-B car to move away from the three cities of Cleveland, Columbus and Cincinnati and back to Chicago, where she could ride out the pandemic in true style, living the high life in her lover's spare condo—downtown, along the Gold Coast.

At least that had been her plan, until her lover Max had pointed out that her car was not technically street-legal and he had concerns about her driving it back to the city.

Jill started to regret sending her lover snapshots of her hoopdie in its total state of disrepair. Initially, she thought he might find it clever that she had skillfully used electrical tape to MacGyver the tailpipe to the bottom of the passenger side door after the exhaust system hangers rusted off. But Max was a serious man who did not find jerry-rigging shit the least bit funny.

To add insult to injury, he had correctly pointed out that her car was probably worth less than he still paid for his Chicago parking spot each month, so it would not be worth the fee to park her car at his place downtown. Instead, he suggested that she sell her car and offered to pay for her to rent a car so that she could return to the city safely.

Jill kindly accepted this offer but secretly loathed the circumstances under which it was made, considering that it forced her to, once again, face the fact that she was poor and Max was a millionaire.

Speaking of millions, Jill knew she had a million things to do that moving day but instead of getting off her ass, she simply parked it on the edge of the bed, slumping over like a lump on a log, staring straight down at her unshaven legs and unkept beaver, and feeling unworthy of love, just like a sad song.

In an attempt to comfort herself, she drew her knees to her chest, and crab-crawled backward, across the bed, to cower in the corner, beneath the kryptonite of her favorite comforter. But no sooner had she done so than the theme song to Jaws rang out on her cell phone, sending chills up and down her spine. Her mother was calling her from one of the other homes she owned, across town.

Jill leaped to her feet, kicked off her shoes, and pulled on her big girl pants because this was the time to make her great escape.

She'd never been good at this whole, confusing, "choose your own adventure" thing that her Irish twin Ian had introduced her to, way back in the day, when they were still kids and used to read books together and play the type of games that actually had them convinced that it *was* possible to choose your own adventure in life.

Jill would keep choosing the same path over and over again

because she kept forgetting the paths she had chosen the times before. This used to irritate Ian so much so that he would complain to their mother about how his twisted sister and how she seemed to be totally lacking in the common sense department until one day he just flat-out refused to play games with Jill altogether. Then, he twisted the knife some more.

"You're not crazy… Are you, sis?"

Ian would often ask her questions like that with his big brain, in a gravely serious manner—almost as if he were projecting his own fears onto her, horrified by the fact that they were both somehow spawn of the same gene pool.

No, that's it. Today is not the day to slip into another depression.

Jill shook herself back to reality and noticed she was craving nicotine, so she grabbed her cell phone and raced down the stairs and into the kitchen, where she yanked open the junk drawer and pulled out three packs of Parliament Lights.

She turned each box on its head, shaking it vigorously until a few loose tobacco leaves spilled out over the laminate countertop. Empty. For the umpteenth time that month, Jill raced outside to hunt for cigarette butts in the backyard.

Just as she was bent over—posing like some tacky lawn ornament, inspecting a half-smoked cigarette that was sitting on the lip of a PBR can that had been left soaking in a ring of snow that was melting into muck everywhere outside—Jill's cell phone rang out again from the bowels of her sloppy sweatpants.

Ignoring the sound, she rolled the butt around between her fingers to see if it was dry enough to light. But before she could fire it up it slipped from her grip and fell into the PBR can, where it got soaked in the same cheap, stale beer that had also been sloshing around in her stomach since… Well before she cried herself to sleep the night before.

"FUCK! FUCK! FUCKITY FUCK!" Jill screamed at the top of her lungs, loud enough to wake up the world. With slumped shoulders, she finally fished out her phone to see the text message that her mother just sent her.

"Swinging by in a few to drop off paint supplies for the basement. Also, I have other projects you can do to pay off the back rent you owe me since your last stimulus check ran out, AND... as soon as the pandemic ends, you are getting a real job!!!"

Yes, of course, her mother would accompany that last sentence with three exclamation points.

Jill frantically logged into her online bank account to see if Max had transferred the funds that she so desperately needed to flee from Ohio but her account still reflected a zero-dollar balance. So she shuffled back inside in her dirty Crocs and waddled up the stairs to search for her keys which she found lying under her bed next to her saucer-eyed cat Dream. Right! She still needed to knock that pussy out for their seven-joint ride back to the city. With practiced movements, she laced some Scooby snacks with hemp and fed them to her fur baby.

With that task off her list, Jill gathered up the garbage bags she had stuffed with her shit and tossed them down the stairs. She took a dump, then dragged the bags outside. She popped the trunk and hurled the bags inside before slamming the trunk shut with both hands, pressing down firmly to make sure that it locked—because it had popped open several times before when she was cruising around town, nearly causing a collision.

Leaning against the back bumper of her beater, she took a moment to catch her breath when suddenly her cell phone sounded off again, only this time it was not her mother.

She scrambled to answer the phone. It was some mechanic she had met at a summer music festival the year before.

"I'll take your car off your hands for a few hundred bucks if you can drive it over to the shop as soon as possible to sign over the title. I told you, right, We buy any car!" Jill hung up before she could tell him that yes, she knew. She had heard that annoying jingle on TV enough times to drive her entirely insane.

Just as Jill ended the call she received a notification from her online bank account indicating that Max had just transferred thousands of dollars into it to cover what he called her "moving expenses."

But after that last phone call, she might not need it all. She could cover any other expenses along the way with the cash that she was about to make selling her clunker! But first, she had to put enough gas in the tank to drive it over to the shop.

Jill was beaming with delight at the sight of all those zeros that Max had transferred into her online bank account. She squealed, now that she finally got her ticket out of Ohio. However, the noise startled Dream, who took off running the moment she screamed, pushing open the screen door to sniff out spring.

"Oh no you don't! Get back here!" Jill insisted as she took off after him, dragging him toward her by his tail before scooping him up in her loving arms to lock him inside her car, so that he could not escape before she had the chance to skip town for good and kiss her past goodbye.

The cat was super mellow and easy to catch, meaning the hemp-laced treats that she had fed him earlier must be working their magic.

Jill reclined in the driver's seat of her getaway car and began to transfer money from her online account into her local bank account so that she could buy gas and cigarettes for the road but she had no idea when the money was actually going to hit her local account so she waited with nervous anticipation. She was hunched over the steering wheel, praying that her car would not run out of gas, when the money hit home.

Coasting down an incline near Cadillac Hill, she passed Mount Peace, the cemetery where freshly dug graves awaited the sick souls of all of those who had died in misery, alone, from Covid, during the deadliest months of the pandemic.

To save others from the roaring of her exhaust, Jill cut the engine before she coasted into the drive-thru at the Circle K to buy smokes and a Slurpee from Andraya, the red-bone who had worked at the gas station for as far back as Jill could remember. But when Jill tried to fire her engine back up, it would not turn over.

Summoning her most adorable doe eyes, Jill glanced up at Andraya who smacked her lips, rolled her eyes back in her head, and shifted the sour apple sucker she was chewing on from one cheek to the other without missing a beat.

Then, she barked at Jill, "Throw it in neutral and step out."

Jill jumped out of the driver's seat immediately, as Andraya flipped the counter-top over, to climb down off her bar stool-shaped throne to enter the drive-thru bay where Jill was standing.

"Step back," Andraya said to Jill who stood on the sidelines, speechless, watching as her friend single-handedly pushed her piece of shit car out of the drive-thru and over to a space that was reserved for free air.

Jill felt fucked and cried out, "What if I can't move my car until later? I was supposed to leave today!"

"Nah, that shit's broke. You really gotta figure yourself out, Jill." said Andraya. "There is no free air!" She shouted back over her shoulder, as she sashayed back inside the drive-thru bay, summoning the next car to pull forward by calling out, "Come on baby! I got you."

Jill felt totally deflated as she climbed back in her car, where she began to air her grievances to a complaints department that did not exist.

Finally, she pulled herself together. She picked up the now sleeping Dream and tucked him away in her NPR tote, which she left dangling from her arm, like an ornament, as she proceeded to pop the trunk to grab all her garbage bags. Whatever happened, she was getting the hell out of dodge.

Jill rooted around in the trunk for what seemed like forever before she realized that she could not possibly carry all of the bags that she had stashed back there. So she lightened her load by randomly selecting one of the bags, which she then slung over her shoulder like Santa Claus before waddling off down the streets in her Crocs and dirty crew socks in order to rent a car.

"Welcome to Hurts So Good!" The unfriendly redneck behind the counter at the car rental place joked as Jill approached him with all of her problems.

"Got a reservation?" The man-child asked Jill before she could even get a word in edgewise.

"Ummmm, Nope!" Jill stood in front of him, with her mouth open, catching flies, until she caught herself and started thinking straight again. Then she said "Look outside, it's a ghost town out there! It's the middle of the pandemic and there is not one fucking car on the road, and it ain't a holiday weekend."

"Sorry ma'am, you gotta have a reservation, them is the brakes!" The redneck bore a shit-eating grin as he hocked a loogie, filled with chewing tobacco, into the unlined trash can at his feet, before he crossed his arms over his chest and jammed his hands up into his armpits with his thumbs sticking straight up in the air.

"It is THOSE, THOSE are the brakes you hill jack!" Jill screamed at the stranger at the top of her lungs. But when she saw him hop on a landline she decided it was time to get the hell out of there before he sniffed his own rotten body odor right off his hand.

"For the love of God and country, where is your sense of decorum?" She screamed at the stranger who winked with his eye and passed gas right in front of her, which really sent Jill flying straight out the front door with nary a rental car to speak of.

* * *

"No, you don't understand!" Jill pleaded with the skinny punk chewing bubble gum behind the counter of another car rental place close by. "Please, I am begging you. I have got to get the fuck out of here! I'll do anything!" Jill's hands were shaking like a leaf when she snapped into full victim mode. "I have nothing left to live for! I hate Ohio. This place is a cesspool of backward nobodies and narcissists. You have to help me!"

"Oh, you're one of them diva types!" The kid spewed at her.

"A diva? Please, I am a real woman. Can't you tell by how pissed the fuck off I am… Stan?" She read the print on his sidewards name tag out loud for the whole world to hear.

"No, I mean one of them drama queens. You know, like some bitchy diva?" He asked her outright with a look of complete sincerity.

"No, but my mother is! She is the only person who will socially distance with me and she's Joan Crawford in the flesh. It's like something straight out of a fucking horror movie, I swear! I mean, this woman is a monster, I tell you. I want her out of my bubble and she is the only one left in it! And now," Jill took a deep breath for the rest of her salvo, "now I'm afraid she is going to lock me in the basement with all the hairy wolf spiders and force me to perform D.I.Y. projects to the tune of zero-sum dollars until the cows came home, all because I owe her back rent. Meanwhile, she is living high on the hog! Please, dude, I can't die in Ohio. I don't belong here!"

"Oh wow, you are like one of those has-been, total-goner Diva types, like that babe from Sunset Boulevard."

"The broad or the dead monkey?" Jill asked him to specify using her best Mae West voice.

They were bonding now, right? Soon the punk-turned-empath would be taking pity on her all because he thought she was some kind of chump that was trying to wake the chimp like that morbid scene from Sunset Boulevard…talk about terrible getaway planning.

As the dude was staring her down with his sad sack eyes, Jill glanced through the spacers in his ears to catch a glimpse of the company's auto rental policy written on the wall, which clearly stated that a major credit card must be on file, in order to book a reservation. How could she find her way around the writing on the wall?

A very stylish Spanish woman, donning a pair of rectangular-shaped golden bamboo earrings that swung hypnotically in the negative space just above her graceful swan neckline, approached the counter from behind the punk.

"How old are you?" The woman asked Jill, with piercing eyes and a true air of curiosity in her raspy voice. Her manager's tag was on full display. Carmella.

Jill stood up straight, and cleared her throat before she responded in a low whisper, so that no one could overhear her, "49."

With a genuine smile, Carmella opened her mouth. "Okay, I see what's happening here," she said. "I'm going to need you to take a seat and cool your jets!" She pointed to a chair clear off at the back of the room with an oscillating fan standing beside it.

With her head low, Jill slumped down in the seat as the fan

beside her blew it's dirty little red, white, and blue streamers all over tar-nation. Surely, she must be in hell, because she could feel the heat rising as she stripped down to her tank top and sank into the metal frame of that unforgiving seat.

Minutes, hours, or days later Jill could smell the manager walk up to her.

"What is that fragrance you are wearing?" She quickly asked as she raised herself up in the chair to sit up straight.

"Hmmmm, It's Valentino's *Coral Fantasy*." The manager's voice buzzed with delight as Jill soaked in every bit of what she was selling.

That sounds especially seductive, Jill thought.

The cool-as-a-cucumber manager, smelling sweet as honey, handed Jill a cone filled with cool filtered water. "You looked thirsty," she said.

"Oh, I am!" Jill responded without hesitation as she gulped the water down like a shot before crushing the cone in her bare hand like a beer can.

"I am so sorry that I snapped, I was having a bad hot flash, mama." She said as she leaned all the way into the fan that was propped up beside her. Fear, desperation, and embarrassment all fought for her attention and the fan's steady stream of air seemed like her only chance to survive the landslide of emotions.

"There is no need to apologize!" The manager leaned over to comfort Jill by placing one well-manicured hand gently on her shoulder. "I can sympathize with what you are going through, believe me! Been there, done that. My hot flashes lasted almost ten long years so I know firsthand about aging as a woman. All I can say is: may you descend into madness with grace and know that you are loved."

The next thing she knew, Jill was cruising down the highway, jamming out to a song called *I Follow Rivers* by Lykke Li. She hit a new high in the luxury sedan that she just scored, out of pity, from the feisty, middle-aged Salma Hayek-hot chingona.

"Slick fucking ride, right?" Jill bragged about her prowess to dream who was too busy dreaming to care so Jill popped on her Goodwill sunglasses, fired up a J, and dropped the moon roof back on that luxury pity ride.

Her long-awaited Sheryl Crow song finally started playing over the Bose stereo system as she approached the final toll on Chicago's south side.

Dream stood up to stretch as the car came to a stop. He then contoured his frame into that familiar hunchbacked U shape that had always been part of his signature post-nap ritual. That same type of cat posture that you see on all those cat crafts for Halloween in Ohio at Joan Ann Fabrics.

Meanwhile, Jill was glancing down at the Girl Scout cookie crumbs that were collected in the folds of her Kelly green John Deere riding hoodie.

"Can you believe this, Dream? This king has finally, after all these years, offered me the keys to one of his castles and I show up dressed like a farmer's daughter? Now, this is unacceptable, even for me!"

Jill struggled to stretch her chicken wing behind the driver's seat to grab an article of clothing out of the only garbage bag she salvaged from her past when Dream raised his long tail up in the air and shook it like a rattlesnake. Then, he projectile-pissed all over the clothes and the dash of that luxury sedan that Jill had less than an hour to return to a specific hotel drop-off location in the city.

THE BEFORE AND AFTER LIFE

The next day Jill woke up face down. As that's the way she liked to fuck, she figured she must have fallen asleep masturbating on her lover's bed the night before. The truth of the matter then became abundantly clear when she spotted her vibrator gyrating in slow motion, flipping and flopping around on the floor beside her, reminding her that she was now a fish out of water.

The last time she could remember masturbating herself to sleep that hard was the day she first met Max. The day after he banged her for the first time, from behind, as he often did. Jill would pretty much let him put it wherever he wanted to, given that she had always been the submissive type. And because she so desperately wanted to believe in fairy tales that always had a happy ending she thought that, if she played her cards right, she would someday be married to this handsome Italian prince who just so happened to be one of the sexiest, smartest, and most successful alpha males on the rise in America.

She used to think that she would be wrapping up her 20s with Max as a parting gift – rocking a brand-new name, a brand-new VW Jetta, and a huge diamond ring delivered to her in that signature robin's-egg-blue box from Tiffany & Co. adorned with that matching blue bow, just like every other Lincoln Park Trixie who had ever lived in Lakeview who dreams of someday owning property along the Gold Coast.

Max.

She summoned up the sound of his deep, dark, Darth Vader-esque voice to her ear. He whispered sweet confessions about all of the kinky things he thought about doing to her body as he licked and then screwed her, with his fat-knuckled furry fingers, from behind, swimming in her sweet juices to satisfy his own primal thirst for total domination. She quivered with delight as she recalled the way he used to manhandle her body and pull her long flaming-red ponytail, as she ground her middle-aged bones against the thickness of his overused mattress.

She was getting ready to cum super hard when suddenly she felt that familiar inferno bubbling up inside of her, indicating that she was experiencing yet another hot flash from which there was no escape. With a sigh, she rolled over onto her back in order to avoid the sweat-soaked sheets that were already sticking to the satin mattress cover.

Jill got up, got high again, and finally got her rocks off on a different piece of furniture before falling back onto her lover's bed eating Dove bars. She felt as if she was approaching a state of complete euphoria.

Inspired by drugs, chocolate, and love for Hollywood, Jill focused on the spotlights that were dangling down from the steel frame that her lover had hanging over his bed. Each light was covered in a fine layer of dust, which made it appear like a soft animated creature with one glass eye, fixed upon her face. Specks of dust broke away, floating in front of the lights in the same way that dust had danced in front of the lenses of an old movie projector on rainy days back when she was a kid, watching movies in the auditorium at grade school.

Where had that dust settled now? Jill asked as she began to wax prolific about things that only seemed to matter in her own enchanted world of make-believe.

Back when Jill was a kid she'd thought that maybe she was the beautiful one, that was until her other sisters came along. She thought that maybe she was going to be a famous model or a ballerina, followed by spotlights wherever she went, but that was her lover's life.

Back then, Jill was beautiful too, she must have weighed one hundred pounds soaking wet, and look at her now, menopausal. She had nothing left to aspire to, because why would she? In a blink of an eye she would be dead because time moved so fast.

She was trying to recall the last time she had stepped on a scale as her weed and chocolate buzz began to wear off, but sadly she could not. She had zero clue what she weighed but she did know that there was a heavy price to pay for letting yourself go in the way that she had. So she swore to God, right then and there, that she was going to make every effort to get in great shape before her lover saw her again.

* * *

The sky was raining umbrellas and the wind was blowing sideways across Lake Michigan on the day that Jill actually felt okay enough to get her shit together in Chicago.

That morning she woke up with spittle and salty tears glued to her flush face. She was sticky, dirty, naked, hungry and Dream was crying out "NEOW," insisting that she feed him immediately.

As she had done so often in these past few weeks, she started fiddling again with the complex panel of dimmer switches. Max was such a nerd. How the hell did he manage to operate the elaborate track lighting system he had installed in his condo. Again, she gave up. She had no idea how she had turned the lights on or off in the bedroom the night before, so she just fumbled around the condo in the dark, naked, feeling her way across the walls to find the kitchen doorway, where she could scarcely see any better since it was bright outside and she did not have her glasses on.

"What day is it?" Jill asked Dream, as she considered scrubbing the cat pee out of her dress in the sink so that she would have something of her own to wear downstairs when she ventured out into the city for the first time in seventeen years. It's cat pee. That smell never comes out she thought to herself. So instead she slipped her hands inside her lover's drawers and felt around their smooth surfaces, searching for something to wear.

The only article of clothing Jill found was an old Batman onesie that was wadded up next to an antiquated Macintosh computer monitor at the back of a walk-in closet.

That actually made complete sense: all men she liked thought they were some kind of superhero. It had all started with the actor she had met and fallen in love with back when they graduated from the same college, in Ohio, who had dragged her along to Chicago so that he could pursue a career in the theater. Of course, that didn't work out because he was very good looking but he was a terrible actor.

But Max...

Jill stepped into the shower as memories of Max flooded her senses all at once. She was so thankful it had not worked out with that first boyfriend of hers because Max was a better catch. Max was better in bed, Max was rich and powerful like Batman and he had all the toys.

Jill slipped into her ex-lover's onesie and fastened the snaps up from the crotch of the garment. It clung to her skin, hugging every crevasse of her curvy frame super snug-like. She sat down on a chair in her lover's den and laced up her neon running shoes before dashing out the door to brave the elements in her new getup, quickly grabbing that garbage bag full of pee-soaked clothes to drop them down the trash chute on the way out.

"Did you bring an umbrella?" Cedrick asked her with a smile so electric it could light up the sun. He was younger than Jill and she thought that he looked *so* handsome every time she saw him in his doorman uniform—which so far had really only been like twice.

"No, sir." Jill shook her head as she blushed behind her Cubs mask.

"Well then, may I offer you this one? You may need it. It is raining pretty hard out there." He winked as he helped her through the door, opening the umbrella above her head as soon as she stepped outside.

"Wow, what service!" Jill said thrilled, if not a bit awe-struck, as she danced through the heavy brass doors at the front of the joint to make her way down the wild and wondrous streets of Chicago. As soon as she crossed the threshold, however, she was taken by storm.

The more Jill had to fight the wind off the lake to take each step, the more serious she became about getting her grocery shopping done really fast. For the first time in years, she was going to be systematic about the way she handled this. She created a list in her head of all the things she needed to buy, playing it over and over again, on a loop, whilst simultaneously trying to remember how far up the street the grocery store was and which side of the street it was actually on.

She held the umbrella out in front of her, using it like a body shield to defend herself against the wind and the flying trash that was blowing at her from ten different directions, as she wandered off up Ohio Street, the name of which she did find a bit ironic, as it made it seem as if she would never escape her past life in that place.

Minutes later, she noticed an elderly woman, wearing sun visors and a rain cap, who appeared to be struggling to shuffle through an automatic door up ahead, on the opposite side of the street. She appeared to be holding onto a walker for dear life as all her grocery bags dangled from the steel frame of it, twisting in the wind and obstructing her legs from advancing forward.

Now, you have got to be one brave old woman to still be living in the city at her advanced age. I think she may be my new shero! Jill fought against traffic to rush across the street in order to help the sweet soul gain her bearings. But when she got there, the old biddy basically told her off. She made it crystal clear that she did not need help and then said something along the lines of 'fuck off and get away from me.' So Jill pretended like she did not hear the old woman on count of the wind and she basically kept it pushing, which is what a city dweller does when someone bitches them out for no good reason.

By the time Jill hit the ground running inside the store, she looked like she had gone through a car wash, minus the car, and she could not remember any of the items she had added to her mental grocery list. So she decided to wing it, as usual.

She should probably stock up on food options, just in case her lover decided to pay her a surprise visit and they worked up an appetite afterward and just wanted to spend all day in bed feeding each other.

And then there was coffee, of course. But wait, how did Max take his coffee? After all of these years, she still did not know the answer to that very simple question. Pretty sad, come to think of it. Should she buy sugar? Should she buy half-and-half, or just grab both, just to be safe? *I know he does like some cream in his coffee*, she smiled to herself as picked up a pint of half and half and gave it a shake.

And what did Max eat for breakfast? She asked herself as she strolled down the aisles, soaking wet, in the mostly empty grocery store. She had always slept in long after he left for work when they first met, but that was nearly two decades ago now. She knew he ate pussy for breakfast but she really could not recall him sticking anything else in his mouth before noon.

Surely the man must eat breakfast, though, otherwise, how does he power that genius brain that he uses to manage all of those complex problems that he has to solve while dealing with those hundreds of thousands of employees he manages across the globe? This thought alone exhausted Jill, so instead she decided to just use her imagination to figure out what her lover ate for breakfast, even though she had never seen him do it.

Suddenly, the sitcom Seinfeld came to mind. *That's it! Smart city men eat cereal for breakfast.* To avoid any further confusion, she decided to load every brand in her cart.

Now, what am I going to eat? Jill was certainly not going to be the one in their long-distance relationship who ate nothing but garbage processed food, so she returned to the produce aisle that she had passed up at the back of the store to load down her cart with the kind of colorful magical healthy foods included in this diet that she imagined all the hot women parading around the city in their freaky cut-off Frankenstein pants and super strappy spider woman sports bras were consuming on the daily.

Jill did not have any girlfriends left in the city to actually ask what they ate to stay trim but she had watched her sisters diet often enough to know that you have to eat the rainbow and drink a shit ton of water to look amazing.

Bok Choy sounded magical, and it appeared to be some sort of lettuce for making sandwiches with. Or perhaps she could treat it like an onion or throw it on a salad or something like that. She also grabbed an artichoke while she was standing in the produce aisle, because why not? Everyone liked artichoke dip, right? And besides, she felt confident that as soon as she figured out how to turn the lights on in her lover's lair, she would find a treasure trove of kitchen gadgets stored there to prepare all kinds of exotic dishes at his place with. Max had always bragged about being an excellent cook and everyone knows you can't fuck up a good meal with high-quality ingredients and the right appliances.

She had this whole grocery shopping thing down to a T! Jill splurged on sweet corn because she knew Max loved to grill out on the condominium's rooftop deck when it was nice out. She also knew that she could seduce him with a cob of corn in her mouth because she had done it before and he went wild.

Max was a meat eater from all the times she could remember him treating her to Tavern on Rush, or Gibson's, or Morton's or some other heavenly new steakhouse he had discovered.

Max preferred a highly marbleized cut cooked medium rare. With a blush, she remembered how he'd scoffed at her the first time he took her to a steakhouse and she tried to order her steak well done. From that point on, she'd only ever ordered her meat medium rare and a little bloody, same as him, as they began to feed off each other's vices.

Hmm… Max used to fuck her quick like a jackrabbit. Speaking of which, she needed new batteries for her vibrator… Or did she, if Max was coming to town?

Jill mentally crossed batteries off her list and turned her nose up at the chips and cheaters section as she passed in front of a barrel full of peaches that were propped up as part of a pie display for Mother's Day at the front of Jewels, the grocery store.

The gash in the peaches reminded Jill that she had better get off her tired aging and flat ass soon and get on that Brazilian butt lift video she bought off Amazon months ago. She knew Max preferred a plump peach but then she recalled that DVD was likely located in one of the garbage bags she had left roasting in the trunk of that hot car the day she deserted it back at that gas station in Ohio.

Let bygones be bygones… She could always ask Max for the money to join a fitness club or a body sculpting class when she was good and ready to make those improvements.

Before she made her way out of the store, she even remembered to pick up some cat food and litter, to prevent her fur baby from crying and shitting all over the condo. With a satisfied grin, she confidently strutted to the check-out, knowing that this time her card would not be declined because now she had real money to spend.

Jill was greeted at the lobby door by someone other than Cedrick and this stranger appeared to be someone important, like the building manager, on account of how he was wearing a high dollar suit and appeared to have what she could only describe as a major stick shoved all the way up his tight ass. And that was exactly who he turned out to be and exactly what he had.

He quickly approached Jill without hesitation, invaded her personal space, as he flung a shawl around her shoulders in order to cover the upper portion of her shaking body as he extended one creepy pasta arm toward her to snatch the soaking-wet umbrella that she was clutching for dear life from the grips of her wet hands.

For a moment, Jill felt honored. But then she realized he was trying to prevent her from dripping raindrops all across his freshly polished-to-a-shine marble floors.

Suddenly, his spine seized up as if he had been pierced at the back of his collar by an invisible fish hook and was dragged backward by the sight of that filthy onesie that she was wearing. Or was it by the way her sagging breasts were hanging from her body like a lumpy sack of potatoes? Hard to say, but he did not seem the least bit impressed by her appearance.

"Excuse me! Miss So and So." He said "It is not at all appropriate to wear that kind of attire in this building" The tall slender man's beady little bat eyes were bouncing all over her body. Too late, it became clear to her that he had said so and so in order to allow her to fill in the blank with her own name.

"Jill," she rushed to answer.

"Jill," he repeated it back to her in a shitty-ass tone as if to mock her very existence. This jerk was clearly devastated by her impoverished appearance so she apologized to him for looking like hell, then disappeared into the maze of the building to brainstorm ways in which to reinvent herself now that she lived on the Gold Coast.

When Jill returned to the safety of her lover's lair she could not help but feel triggered by that shitbird manager's knee-jerk reaction to her wayward appearance. She knew that the sight of her frightened the viewer, but goddamn! *A girl's got to eat and I have not even had time to scout out the laundry room yet, so give me a break!*

She shook her head as she put away the groceries and went back to imagining how she and Max would enjoy them together when her lover finally got around to flying into town.

She spent the remainder of the afternoon composing a sticky-sweet email to him, listing all the reasons why she felt that she needed a new wardrobe—starting with the fact that she did not have one. The email was about a novel and a half long when she finally hit send. She thought surely it would take him some time to pore over every detail of it and review all the expenses she had carefully itemized, so imagine her shock when moments later the funds she had requested in the subject header of her carefully crafted email quickly appeared in her online account, no questions asked.

This generous act of kindness was unrivaled by anything that Max had done for her before. So Jill knew beyond a doubt that she'd be eternally grateful to him, from this day forward and for the rest of her life for all the things that she imagined he would give her.

Now I don't have to worry about anything. Finally, I can have it all! And who wouldn't want this lifestyle? She closed her eyes, fell back onto her lover's bed, and just let go of all her worries for once. "You see?," she told Dream, before exhaling deeply for the first time in forever, "This is why Max is perfect." She continued to muse about Max while the jazz played out of the speakers of his expensive house stereo. "Nobody told him that I was special. He decided. Nobody told him to spoil me rotten. He just wants to take care of me. He chose me."

Tired of talking, Jill continued in her head. Because to be fair, it hadn't all just been Max, of course. This was also due to her seductive superpowers, which in the past she had used as a skill to survive during the times when she felt like she could not take care of herself. But now she was going to hone those special skills of seduction once again, in order to elevate herself to a level where she might be considered worthy of experiencing a lifestyle that she knew he could afford to provide her with.

Jill was busy thanking Max for the money he just sent her and just kissing his ass in general when she recalled how earlier she had been standing in that hoity-toity grocery store, embarrassed because she had no idea how the love of her life took his coffee. She considered asking him but in the end, she opted not to bother because she knew that he had better things to do with his valuable time than to answer trivial questions about his breakfast rituals.

She'd have to be careful about the questions she'd ask him. So a brainstorm was in order. If she could only ask him one question, period, what would it be? And would he even take the time out of his busy day to answer it?

She just had to know and so she typed: "Who is your favorite movie star?" She was shocked when he texted back right away.

His initial response was unacceptable, she didn't look

anything like his crush. But when he told her his number two pick, Jill knew that she could transform herself into the other woman, over time.

THE MONKEY IN HER PURSE

Sasha Tara may have been younger than Jill but they did look an awful lot alike, even Jill's sisters told her she looked like Sasha Tara who was an up-and-coming Irish-American movie star who had red hair just like Jill, so she could definitely look like Max's second choice.

To get to a place where Jill could fit into the kind of fashion that Sasha Tara wore, she quickly made a zero-carb sandwich out of that Bok Choy she bought at the grocery store, feeling good about how she was taking charge of her life again. However, it tasted like garbage when she bit into it so she spit it out and washed it down the garbage disposal, opting for pizza instead.

Compared to Ohio, in Chicago, she had so many pizza places to choose from. She might order a party-cut pizza from Lou Malnatis, the way the corners curled up was amazing, and their toppings were super delicious. Or maybe Roberts would be better. Their brick oven pie from River East had the best crust in town. No, it would have to be Giordano's tonight, with its thick and buttery brick oven flavor, filled with that firm garlic cheese and topped with the chunkiest zesty and tangy tomato sauce.

When she woke up from her pizza coma the next day, her body was making stuffing out of the crumbs left over from her binge.

She stood up, dusted herself off, and stumbled into the kitchen to make coffee. It was then she realized she had forgotten to buy filters. Plus, there was no coffee maker to be found.

For the first time since she arrived at the condo, she opened all the cupboards up, only to discover they were bare. And when she turned to face the floor-to-ceiling kitchen windows, she noticed there was a workout room located directly across from her and

there was a whole row of men, running on treadmills over there, waving in her direction.

She quickly ducked for cover when it dawned on her that she was standing there, naked as a jaybird, completely on display for all of them to see. Crouching for cover, she dashed back into the bedroom to find something to put on.

When she had peeled that wet rag of a onesie off her smelly cat body the day before, she had thrown it in the trash along with her cat-pee-soaked dress, so she needed something new to wear. After a quick look around, she ripped the blood-red satin sheets from her lover's bed to fashion them into a toga, by tying it off at the waist with a dog leash she found dangling off a loose hook in the back of a coat closet. Did Max own a dog? The leash looked brand new but she had only ever known Max to be a cat lover.

For a second, she considered texting him: "Do you have a dog now?" But she shut down the idea of asking him yet another silly question like that pretty quickly. Her lover was a very busy man. After all, he lived in Manhattan—that bustling Metropolis to the east where everything moved at the speed of sound. He oftentimes reminded her that since he had made it more than ten years there he could make it anywhere which made Jill feel honored to somehow still be part of his amazing life.

Jill knew she had to shop for clothes soon but the thought of all those harshly lit public dressing rooms in all those off-the-rack sort of shopping experiences made her freak out. She'd definitely need to be a little bit more mellow for that kind of outing.

Luckily, she still had the last of her Ohio stash of weed, which she smoked up before she made her way out the door. Yes, she was going to shop eventually. But first things first, she had to replenish her weed supply at the local dispensary, where she was going to purchase it legally and smoke it on the streets, for the first time ever in her life.

When she arrived at her destination on Clark street in River North, a car pulled up to ask the security guard, who was standing next to her, if they had any reservations left for the night. They must have mistaken the joint for some high dollar restaurant or something, until the security guard blew them off as he took another drag off his lit cigarette.

Before Jill could figure out how to get thru the door, some haughty and snobbish-looking chick approached the same security guard coming at her from the opposite direction.

"Ummmm yeah, hi, I'm Karen and I'm here to like, you know, buy weed," she whispered into his ear, loud enough for the whole city to overhear, while she giggled to herself as if anyone might find her cute or charming.

"Well, it looks like a few guys beat you to it Karen." He pointed to the back of the line which ended at the beginning of the next city block. Jill popped on her shades and followed Karen to the back of the line.

At the first stop inside the dispensary they scanned her I.D. and asked her if she had placed an online order, to which Jill naturally responded, "No." With big eyes, she looked around, taking in this entirely new world she'd entered into. This was her first time in a weed store, so she had no real concept of what she was doing, how many different strains of weed there actually were in the world, or what in the world their purpose was. This part of her new life adventure was truly fascinating and she hung on every word that the shop clerk spoke as they shared information with her.

Finally, for the first time in her life, she was getting a proper education on cannabis and the ways in which it could be used to heal her soul and help her function like a normal human being, even with depression, so that she could get shit done in life, just like everybody else. Being fully functional was Jill's number one priority when it came to managing her mental illness and those dreaded night terrors that she had suffered from, ever since she was a kid, that were due to circumstances and PTSD which were beyond her control.

As soon as the weed vape was handed to her, Jill eagerly ripped into the fun foil packaging surrounding her soon-to-be sanity and pulled down her mask to take a puff. But suddenly she found herself face-to-chest with a much younger male security guard, a very tall man with broad shoulders.

"You can't vape inside the store," he said, as he escorted her outside as quickly as possible. When she 'accidentally' bumped into his side on the way to the door, she could feel he was packing heat, which truly turned her on. She could totally imagine how that fine young tenderloin would just put his hands all over her if she was frisked by him but he never did that. Instead, he just told her to keep it moving, so she slipped her cheap gas station shades back on over her bloodshot eyes and stepped out onto the sizzling sidewalk before sauntering down the street on a dream-like stroll, casting long shadows onto the bubble gum-stained sidewalks as she crossed over Clark Street right in front of a row of cop cars, blowing weed in the wind.

For the first time in months, Jill burst out laughing spontaneously. Was this the best day of her life or what? She had to pinch herself because she was actually smoking weed in public places, outside, without hiding it and with no sense of shame. And from the moment she took her first hit off that vape pen, she felt herself falling in love with the city where she fell in love with Max all over again.

With her arms wrapped around herself in an affectionate

embrace, she spun around in circles, staring straight up at the sky as if there were a camera hanging overhead with a bird's eye view of her new perfect life as Sasha Tara, her own fantastic version of Barbie.

She was lost in a haze of happiness when she spotted golden arches up ahead, which certainly indicated to her brain that it was time to chow down. She grabbed a few sandwiches and plopped down on a bench and started stuffing her face. But Jill was nothing if not a multi-tasker. What's more, she was on a mission! So she whipped out her new cell phone and feverishly tapped away on it until she found a Marshalls store nearby.

By the time Jill hit the department store's revolving door she was as high as a skyscraper. The glass blades in the door were spinning so fast that she felt like she was getting the run-around—they spun her in circles thrice before spitting her out inside the store. What the door didn't spit out, however, was her toga, which got stuck on that continuous glass loop. For a second, Jill was in a tug-of-war with the fucking thing, until the toga was finally yanked clean from her body in such a swift, downward-pulling motion that it sent her spinning across the floor, where she came to a halt splayed out in her birthday suit and the only things left covering her was the mask on her face and the dog leash, that she had used as a belt, that was still strapped around her waist.

Jill hadn't yet found the clarity to stand-up, when an odd-looking stranger approached her wearing a store smock with no name tag. Still, Jill assumed the woman worked for the store since she was toting around a whole mess of plastic Marshalls bags, which she proceeded to stick to Jill's sweaty skin to cover her up her lady bits.

"Holy Shit! Now *this* is the most embarrassing thing that has ever happened to me! This is like my worst fucking nightmare… Oh My God! Thank you so much! How can I ever repay you for your kindness?" She asked the odd stranger as she scrambled to her feet.

"Seven cents each bag," the stranger said to Jill. "Cash only!" she added, holding out her hand as she waited to be paid.

"*Seven cents* for a plastic bag? Now *that* is total rip off!" Jill exclaimed. "Who the hell pays for a plastic bag?"

"Everyone in Chicago, you fucking tourist! Now, do you want these bags or not?" The stranger asked without smiling. She waited only one second before she started to snatch the bags back by plucking them from Jill's skin one by one until she was left standing there in her birthday suit.

"NO! Wait! Come back with those!" Jill called after the mysterious character as she flattened her body, just like one of those working stiffs from the Beetle Juice movie, as she faded into the fabric of the city by slipping through a small sliver of a crack in the concrete wall.

Jill turned around to face the music with her hands covering her privates, when lo and behold she spotted a second store clerk coming her way. This stranger was smiling a welcoming smile as she approached Jill with open arms holding out a beautiful satin white bathrobe for her to wear.

As Jill slipped her arms into the robe, this store clerk said: "Hi, I'm Cami, I thought you could use some assistance."

"Oh what luck!" and "you must be an angel," Jill complimented Cami before she closed her eyes to pretend that she had just been swept away in a fabric softener commercial as she snuggled up to the silky-soft material on the white robe by rubbing her cheeks against the soft fabric. She then tied it off at the waist, in a loop D loop motion as if she was about to gift herself to the luckiest man alive.

A twirl in front of the mirror made her fall in love with the robe even more. On the back of it was printed the word BRIDE, plain as day.

"Oh, wow!" Jill said "Just imagine... me a bride, at my age!"

"Sure, why not!" Cami insisted. Grabbing Jill's arm as she gently guided her deeper into the store, where fabrics of all different textures brushed up against her body.

"So what can I help you with today?," Cami asked with another kind smile, "all the basics I imagine?"

Jill spent the rest of the afternoon shopping with Cami. They danced around the store picking out dresses that they thought would look super cute on Jill and she tried them on. These were not the kinds of dresses that she would have selected for herself at all but the crazy part was that every single outfit Cami picked out for her to try on, fit her like a glove. Jill was thrilled with Cami's selection, in the end, and so she bought everything she picked out.

Standing at the register, Jill reached over her shoulder, as if she was cupid grabbing an arrow that was about to pierce a man's heart as she popped the tag off the back of her favorite new wrap around dress. The dress was a rich plum color because Cami had said that jewel tones complimented her stunning blue eyes. Plus, Jill fancied the way that dress hugged every inch of her body without revealing anything too X-rated up top and also it was made of a super breathable, cotton type fabric.

I need to vamp out and buy some deep purple lipstick to complete this look, she thought. So as soon as she left the department store, she skipped down the street to Sephora.

The last time she was at this all things beauty shop, Jill had noticed something curious about the effect that the monochromatic beauty superstore had on all the females in Chicago. For some odd reason, women refused to believe that this particular place was never not open. She would watch as the customers would fly into the revolving doors even though they never budged before 11 a.m. But that never stopped people from trying to get into the place moving at the speed of Kamikaze jet fighters as they catapulted their bodies into the revolving glass doors to no avail. Luckily, thanks to her detours this morning, the time was 11:11 on the dot when she arrived.

With her new lipstick on point, Jill sashayed through patches of sunshine on her way back to the condo as she began to think about her future with Max. *You know...,* She said to herself, *he has helped you turn your whole life around! So the least you can do in return is to get in great shape. Honestly, if you just pick up your pace and walk a little faster every day, and stop eating pizza you could be the woman of his dreams again.*

* * *

Her breakfast drag from her disposable vape was barely hitting anymore and she was sucking on it really hard too. Knowing it had run out of puff power, she switched over to the Sativa flower she'd bought the day before, which, the clerk had explained to her, had a much higher percentage of THC than any weed that she had likely ever smoked before in her life. She cooked it up in a glass pipe, inhaling its essence. The effects were almost instant.

"Walgreens, Walgreens... Walgreens rhythms with magazines, greens and zines!" With a giggle, she looked around to see if Dream liked her brainstorms as much as she did. As he looked entirely unimpressed, she insisted: "There can't be many things that rhythm with greens and zines and I can rhythm like that totally fucked up. That must mean that I am some kind of stable genius, or do you think I am simply mad?" She asked her cat.

She continued to pontificate over the importance of rhyming while high when she stopped to grab a cappuccino, and only a cappuccino from McDonald's—because she was currently on a caffeine-rich diet that consisted of nothing more than booze and coffee, as of late, in order to lose weight.

I'm not so different from all the other humanoids around here, walking around with masks on, holding a coffee cup on a hot spring day, she thought. *And all humanoids prefer their morning rituals, whatever they*
may be.

She only wished that she had two hot glazed donuts fresh from Krispy Kreme's drive-thru, first thing in the morning, after the gym, like she had back in Ohio, to go with her current zero-calories-before-noon purely liquid diet.

She was sucking down the rest of cappuccino numero duo when she waltzed into Walgreens, belching up milk bubbles, in order to find some magazines that she could use as inspiration to turn herself into Sasha Tara. With her purse filled with every magazine that showcased the actress, she returned to Marshalls to show Cami the lady that she aspired to become. Cami had proven she had an eye for fashion so naturally the salesclerk could help her transform herself into the woman of her lover's dreams.

Cami had no clue who Sasha Tara was but once Jill showed her photos of the celebrity in Vibe magazine, she instantly knew the kind of look Jill was going for.

"Come on, let me show you our shoe selection," she said.
Cami pulled out a fantastic array of women's heels in a variety of colors and styles. Jill found a pair of purple pumps that perfectly matched the plum dress that she had purchased there the day before. The only setback was that there was only one shoe in the box so together she and Cami scoured the shelves, like a couple of amateur sleuths, searching high and low for that missing purple pump. "Ah- ha!" She declared. "There you are! She snatched up the missing shoe which she had found sitting in a different box, crammed under the shelf, at the end of the aisle.

Jill was so pumped about her new purchase, but she chose to wear her running shoes to the south side, to the salon Cami sent her to so that she could take her nails to the next level.

She had only been to the south side on one other occasion, years ago, when Max took her to Soldiers field to catch a Bears game. But now the field was empty and bore a name that she did not recognize and all the players were long gone.

Jill had a Lyft driver drop her off as close to the salon as he could. The neighborhood Jill found herself standing in looked nothing like any part of the city that she had ever seen before. A majority of the businesses were shuttered, boarded up, and left abandoned. There were empty liquor bottles strewn all over the city streets.

But The Perfect Set was an oasis of a salon in an otherwise desolate ghost town. It was super clean inside and she was instantly greeted by Fang, a friend of Cami's.

"You come highly recommended!" Jill flashed her million-dollar smile at Fang, who graciously smiled back.

Fang poured Jill a tall glass of refreshing cucumber-infused water and kindly handed it to her before leading her to an overstuffed chair that was mounted on an elevated platform in the center of a great room. From this throne, Jill had a full view of this wall of glowing tiles that gradually changed colors to match the lights that were glowing from within the bubbling foot bath that she was soaking her barking dogs in, as Fang lined up his tools with the precision of a surgeon.

In the entrance area, water was falling from a spinning glass ball, and giant jade statues were planted alongside lush bright green tropical trees that appeared to be flourishing under the many multiple natural light sources, including the row of skylights that were allowing the sun to shine down on that happy space. The place reminded Jill of a sculpture garden, which made her want to meditate or practice not talking, while she drank that refreshing water.

After Jill picked her color, Fang let her settle in as he removed her running shoes and began to gently rub her aching arches.

"If your feet are happy, you will be happy," Fang said to her, while she settled into silence to let the colors of the rainbow and all that natural light wash over her soul.

This is what meditation was like, right?

Fang peered back and forth between an over-sized magnifying glass and the magazines Jill had brought in, in an effort to meticulously replicate the pattern on the set of nails that Sasha Tara displayed in her engagement photos.

Back at the condo, after an exhausting day of self-care and shopping, Jill ordered Grub Hub and rented every movie Sasha Tara starred in so that she could study the kind of intimate apparel the celebrity wore in her sex scenes.

What started out as research, however, soon turned into a soft-core porn fantasy for Jill when she noticed that one of the celebrities commingling with Sasha Tara happened to look an awful lot like Max. She masturbated with all of her might until she burned out the motor in her vibrator and decided to just start go at it the old-fashioned way, by using her hands to manually rub one out. She brought herself to climax six or seven times in a row before she finally had enough excitement for one night.

The next day, Jill returned to a red rubber track she had spotted the day before. It was the exact color of the red carpet at the Oscars and was surrounded by gold and black benches that were resting on sunny patches of grass in the middle of a picturesque park like an oasis of peace in the middle of it all. She was wearing her new purple pumps to practice her movie-star walk while she jammed out to a playlist she created on YouTube.

I should really learn how to use Spotify at some point.

After a while, she decided to pick up her pace and walk just a little faster—all part of her weight-loss plan. She was rounding the final bend on that magical red carpet ride when she stepped down on her ankle instead of her foot, causing her to topple over sideways, right in front of a handsome Latino stranger who happened to be sitting on the closest park bench chewing on a burger wrapped in a white paper bag.

He leaped to his feet to help her so fast that the burger went flying right out of his hands, freeing up both of his beautiful buff arms to come to her rescue.

Jill had never witnessed a man so fine, in his crisp white tank top and form-fitting red drawstring shorts that were clinging to the tight little curls growing in tufts along his beefy, thick thighs.

As he was raising her up, she caught a whiff of the cologne that he was wearing and she thought he smelled like someone she wanted to fuck.

"Waste of a good burger," Jill joked.

"Never mind that," He said, "I think I'm hungry for something else now." He smiled at her chest, as if her hills had almond shaped eyes.

Days passed before Jill returned to the track to practice her runway walk again but somehow she managed to make it back there before that week ended.

She was singing along to There She Goes by the La's, gazing out at the boats sailing along the lakefront, as she rounded the last loop of the red rubber track. She was strutting her stuff with all the chutzpah that she could muster when suddenly she began to feel like everything was closing in on her. She began to feel faint and then she passed out.

What she saw when she came to her senses was that hot Latino stranger dangling an all-beef hot dog above her wrapped in foil with a poppy seed bun.

She had collapsed in exactly the same spot where she'd landed the last time she'd tried to make it around the track and once again the Latino was there to save the day.

He was dangling a water bottle below the waistline of his skivvies for her to grab, though Jill felt like grabbing something else.

"You must be thirsty," He said. "I think you passed out, actually." He placed a warm hand, the size of a catcher's mitt, over the small of her lower back, cradling her in his arm to offer her the support her body needed.

"I may be wearing my bra too tight," she suggested as she gazed into the glowing haze of his muddy brown eyes with their long curled lashes.

"Maybe you should take it off." He suggested.

Completely distracted by thoughts of sex, Jill spent the next few days spread-eagle on her lover's lounge, watching erotic scenes while she played with the red hot new vibrator she purchased at the Hustler Hollywood store on Clybourn. It was rechargeable so she never had to worry about burning out the batteries again.

"Fuck me!" Jill said as she grabbed her new toy by the horns, riding it hard before it fell to the floor wet, right before she passed out beside it.

The following morning Jill was still feeling those good vibes, though she'd decided she really had to do something about the whole passing-out in the middle of the day thing. That's why she strolled into Nordstrom on the Mag Mile to shop for bras that fit her the way that bras should.

She began her search by flagging down a sales associate, a sweet honey named Harlow. As Jill explained her situation to the retail assistant, she started pulling her shirt up over her head to check what size bra she was wearing, earning her a side-eye from that sweet honey. After a lot of twisting around, Jill decided to pull her shirt off, but when she finally had her bra size question answered, Harlow was nowhere to be found.

Jill scanned the store before she spotted her again. Harlow was standing next to the fitting rooms, dangling a bunch of bras from her fingertips as if she was waiting for Jill to get with the program.

Inside the fitting room, Jill turned around to face the door as Harlow began to toss half a dozen bras over the top of it for her to try on.

Wow, she works fast! Jill thought as she pulled the bras down off the door to examine the styles and sizes that Harlow had selected for her to try on.

"Quad D cup?" Jill snorted out loud as she examined the label on the band of the first bra. "Wait, this is not my size. Why are all these bras a Quad D cup?"

Jill was just standing there, in a state of utter shock, when Harlow's matter-of-fact voice came through the door.

"Just try one on."

Jill was downright flabbergasted to find that the red lace bra fit her perfectly and that she did, in fact, wear a much larger cup size than she initially thought. That was a nice little fact to share with Max later!

When Jill stepped out of the changing room to show how perfectly her new bra fit, Harlow looked entirely unimpressed.

"You know, most women wear the wrong bra size because

they never bother to have a proper fitting done at a department store that offers the wide range of sizes like we do. You should have come in sooner. Now, go on and try on the others."

After that uplifting experience, Jill bounced her boobies straight into Sephora, to treat herself to the ultimate makeover, just for fun.

The forlorn licensed beauty advisor was aggressively rubbing makeup off Jill's face with a cotton round that was rapidly disintegrating. Apparently, she didn't get the memo on the fun she was supposed to be having.

"Who needs makeup when we have no place to go? And how sad is that? Everything has been canceled. Weddings, concerts, parties! We have nothing to look forward to anymore," She spoke through her colorless cotton mask.

Thankfully, she was soon escorted away by a second, far more experienced cast member, in costume, who had quickly appeared on stage to usher out her Debbie Downer counterpart.

"What is this, some sort of sad sack rendition of 'send in the clowns,' for Christ's sake? Our clients do not want to be subjected to all this negative Nelly nonsense!" The director whose nameplate read Wheatley insisted, as she approached Jill to take center stage, holding a shiny white acrylic palette in her hand that was covered in the most electrifying jewel tones that Jill had ever laid eyes on.

The director's eyes were brushed with the bright shades of the sun in fields of golden glitter with amber accents, used to accentuate the radiance of her rich, dark-mocha skin.

"First we need to tidy up those messy brows." She insisted.

Her own brows were flawless. Wheatley bore the blades of Grace Jones and the skills of a surgeon as she hypnotically swirled a stick around in her honey pot before applying a warm, thin strip of it, evenly and with a steady hand, to Jill's unruly arches. Instantly, Jill's status was elevated from Eugene Levy to Lauren Bacall, with one fell swoop of a stick.

Wheatley sat down very close to Jill with her metallic-colored face mask on. She carefully studied Jill's almond-shaped eyes as she gently applied a Cleopatra black to their slightly upturned ends, after shading the lids with a fine dash of Cobalt and Kingfisher blue. The look reminded Jill of high school, when she had rocked out to The Bangles as she walked like an Egyptian down the city streets as the light from a fading sun shone upon her sun-kissed face.

With her eyebrows perfectly arched and heading back to her king's castle, Jill tried to relive that magical moment from the 1980's by snapping photos of herself dancing around and from every possible angle, so that she could seduce her lover with her carefree spirit later on.

When she got inside, she whipped off her top and began snapping photos of herself in her new bras, seducing the camera with her colorful eyes as she made love to the lens until she was satisfied with the results.

She snapped centerfolds worthy photos of herself spread eagle on her lover's marble-topped dining room table, under the wooden beams with crystal fixtures attached that now shone down on her body, which was lit up like a Christmas Tree in July.

She did shots of herself in the kitchen, wearing his favorite shade of blood red, while she sucked off a banana.

She soaked herself in coconut oil, that stripper kind that had been recommended to her by none other than the 'queen of everything under the sun that is not garbage' at the drugstore, that the original skinny girl cocktail creator, Bethenny Frankel.

Jill rubbed the lotion all over her skin with vigor, activating the kind of heat which made her feel like crawling across her lover's bearskin rug—buck naked, in the dark, fire roaring, with her ass straight up in the air like a cat in heat, as she grazed the tippy top of the fur pelt with her nipples while her tongue was in full wag-the-dog mode and the flames of Maui filled her ocean-colored eyes as if she had the power to envision the future.

Jill thought those photos were the vibe so after the sunset, she spent hours editing them down to select only the best of the best. She had recently watched The Idol on MAX, so she knew what kind of savage love look she was going for and boy did she nail it.

"I should have gone pro as a photographer *and* a model for Hustler," she told Dream.

She stayed up all night dreaming about her future with Max as she cropped this and threw a filter on that photo. Finally, there were the ones where she playfully rolled around in the rose petals she had scattered across her lover's bed because she was trying to go for that ultimate centerfold shot. The kind of shot that lands you the life of your dreams.

"Less is more. LESS. IS. MORE!" She kept telling herself over and over again as she made the final selection of sexy snaps to tempt her lover with.

Moments after she sent the photos, she received a text notification and her heart skipped a beat, but the message was not from her lover. It was from one of the many employers she had worked for back in Ohio. They were hounding her to return to work since Weekend at Bernie's had predicted months back that the pandemic was already over, even though the media was consistently wrong about everything.

Later that same afternoon Jill again jumped on her phone, only to find a second notification from the same employer, talking about some ridiculous fucking opportunity that they wanted to offer her in a state where she never wanted to work or live in the first place.

By the end of the day her phone was about to die so she plugged it in while she eagerly waited for her lover to respond to the sexy snapshots that she sent. She was pacing back and forth while she tried with all her might to convince herself that the only reason why he did not respond right away had to have something to do with the time difference.

Jill had chain smoked every last cigarette left in the carton she bought, taken an entire six-pack of White Claw to the face, and re-smoked every last chunk of Cheeba she could find in her bowl before the voice in her head returned to haunt her again in real life.

COME TO CALL

When she caught herself engaging in yet another self-deprecating dialogue, Jill knew that the devil had come to call. For years, it had been putting her down over and over again, trying to convince her that she was a total waste of space.

This time Jill was determined not to let the devil win. This time she was going to fight that voice every step of the way. She was going to tackle it head-on because she was no longer going to let that evil spirit keep her from finding the happiness she deserved, not this time around.

This time she was going to get the kind of love that she knew she deserved because she had the heart of an angel. She knew she walked in God's good graces and she was worthy of that flavor of love in her life.

All of these thoughts were going through Jill's head as she was seated outside Rumba, her favorite new coffee shop. But suddenly, her self-empowerment was rudely interrupted by a hot flash, which caused her to start obsessively scrolling back through the selfies she'd sent to Max the night before because he had not responded to her yet. She was zooming in on each one of them separately to ensure that she did not forget to edit out any of her known flaws-a-plenty.

She examined every detail with the magnifying tool as she compared them to the screenshots she had taken of Sasha Tara, when EUREKA! She stumbled upon the reason why Max may not have responded to her glamour shots. With a baffled expression, she dropped her cell phone into the crack between her thighs.

"That is it! It's my hair! Of course!" Jill grabbed a generous chunk of her fiery locks between her fingers, before she picked her phone back up to uncross and then cross her fit legs again.

Sasha Tara really only had very long hair at the beginning of her career, back when she was a nobody. Then she said all that stupid shit on social media that ruined her career and she had to reinvent herself like the Phoenix rising from the ashes would—or in my case, the ashy skin. That long hair look was worn by her long before she discovered her signature style, which has always been the pixie cut! It would be ridiculous to think that Sasha Tara would ever grow her hair out again. Just like Halle Berry would never consider going back to any length of hair after she found out she looked so drop-dead gorgeous when she got it all cut off.

With her course of action all figured out, Jill went back to her new friend, the director and make-up artist Wheatley, at Sephora, for advice.

Wheatley passed her off to a neighbor, named Hector, for the perfect pixie cut. It seemed that all the stars aligned because Jill was able to book an appointment with this hair stylist right away.

She brought along her NPR bag stuffed full of all her magazines, pulling them out, one by one, in an attempt to try and show them to Hector. But he was not having any of that nonsense.

"Don't worry honey. For you? I have the perfect pixie!"

Jill observed as Hector picked up a black mass of fabric, from the rolling station next to him, and shook it out in front of her, on the floor, spreading her hair all over the place, after he chopped it all off.

"Do you mind sweeping that up?" Jill asked promptly but in the politest way possible, as Hector re snapped the cape around her neck, only tighter this time, like a John Wayne Gacy garrote, in order to fix the parts of her hair that were uneven.

"Excuse me! I do not take orders!" Hector drew out his dramatic response as he backed up, shaking his finger at Jill's reflection in the mirror, as if he were speaking to the Hyde side of her Jekyll.

She could tell that he was offended so she quickly offered up an explanation, even though she was struggling to speak. "No, you don't understand. It is for a good reason. I swear!" She swallowed hard as she crossed her heart hoping to die, like a child, insisting that she was not trying to boss that queen around, as she stared up at him through innocent eyes.

She had just witnessed the stylist completely transform himself, right in front of her face, from Hector into a far more effeminate and nefarious version of himself with a hot temper, diva type tendencies, and unsteady hands for cutting. This new Hector spun her right around in that chair, grabbed his scissor blades again, and went to town by chopping her hair even shorter.

Nervously, Jill closed her eyes and swallowed, praying to God that he was capable of giving her a flattering haircut this time.

When the blades stopped slicing the space above her head, Jill could not face herself in the mirror, so she cast her gaze down at the floor instead. It felt like she had just been burned at the stake somehow, as she sat there, robed of her stolen beauty, surrounded by a ring of fire, that was very much of her own making.

Hector grabbed a broom and swept the mixed clippings up quickly before Jill even had a moment to form an opinion about what he had done to her hair. He dumped the clippings in a plastic bag, put a knot in the top, handed the bag to Jill, and then straight out of the clear blue sky said,

"You look like the kind of woman who carries a monkey around in your purse," with no follow-up explanation given.

Jill had no clue what the hell he was talking about, especially since she rarely carried a purse, but she did know one thing for sure: There was no way in hell she was ever returning to Hector for a haircut!

Jill tried to fix her hair and meticulously apply layers of makeup to her face before she could take new selfies to send to Max in the morning. He responded to the photos right away.

"You cut off all your hair? Why? I liked it better long."

Devastated, Jill collapsed on his couch. It was going to take such a long time to grow her hair back the way it was. She'd been such a fool for taking such drastic measures to cut it all off in the first place and without a full understanding of what her lover actually wanted her to look like. Jill was starting to feel like a total failure at the only thing she had aspired to do since she'd set foot in that concrete jungle and that was to please her lover.

"Time for plan B. And it certainly won't be the first time I said *that* to Max," Jill confessed to Dream. Then, she threw back her head and chose to laugh instead of cry, as she loaded a glass one-hitter with some hybrid lemon meringue kush, the number six by Cresco, as she preferred to fade into the city scenery rather than face reality.

THE MONKEY ON HER BACK

Jill lost track of time like that fuck boy having an affair with Mrs. Robinson in the movie The Graduate. The summer months slipped by, while she spent her days drunk and high. She'd been rejected by her lover for a former version of herself, or because he found someone else more attractive, which always seemed to be the way it was with fucking men.

Jill, however, refused to remain bitter, instead striving to be best. Besides, Max was still covering all of her living expenses and even though he had not contacted her, she had still carried on living in his castle. Because what the hell else was a scared-shitless, out-of-shape, starving artist from Ohio supposed to do with her time two years into a raging pandemic that had torn her family apart, killed at least a million people in America alone and turned the city she loved into a ghost town—where Mary was now being hailed more often than any cab?

Mary Gold, of course! Why didn't I think of her sooner…

Mary Gold had been Jill's mentor. She wrote "Taken By Storm," the first adult romance novel that Jill ever read and the very same book that had inspired her to become a writer herself, only now there was no time like the present.

She dialed up Mary, by heart, from the seat on her lover's throne as she smoked her last cigarette and tinkled into the toilet, releasing all the corpse gas and toxins from her totally tortured middle-aged body.

When Mary did not answer Jill left her a message to call back as she sprawled out on the couch with the remote control in hand.

While waiting for the call, Jill spent her time obsessively

tugging at the tufts of her short, frizzy red hair, willing it to grow out faster then it possibly could whilst binge-watching the Real Housewives of Atlanta. She had convinced herself that this show was somehow research for her future life as one of the Real Housewives of Chicago, when she would spend all the money the producers gave her pursuing her dreams while looking fabulous doing so.

Her reverie was cut short by the ringing of her phone: finally, Mary called her back via the video app. Jill scrambled to find the device, which she eventually did, with her hair sticking straight up in the air due to her messing with it so much.

"Say, that reminds me to pick up more troll dolls for bingo." Mary made a snide remark.

"Excuse me?" Jill scratched her head as her mentor quickly walked off camera.

"I should add that to my to-do list." Mary had said without so much as a hello in order to ease the blow.

"Hello?....Mary? Is there anybody out there?" Jill asked in an obtuse, sad-sack sort of way, as she leaned in toward the screen on her cell phone, tilting her head in different directions as if she were inspecting the smallest details of a tiny house.

All of a sudden Mary popped back up on screen with a notebook and pen in her hand so Jill jerked the screen back, away from her face.

"Oh Mary! There you are! I missed you! So tell me, how have you been? I have not seen you in so long?"

"Divorced," said Mary.

"Oh, I am so sorry to hear that."

"Well, I am not!" Mary chuckled. "After all, I am starting such an exciting new chapter in my life. I am in love again!" She proclaimed with a great sense of joy.

After a while, Jill grew tired of listening to Mary carry on about some catfish she had met on Instagram and so she quickly changed the subject.

"I will never forget the day you signed my copy of Taken by Storm at that young author's conference where we met Mary. That meant everything to me. I really mean it.

"Did you ever finish the sequel?" She asked.

"Oh heavens no. That was decades ago! And besides… business is booming and I never turn down work! I have copywriting jobs coming out of the woodwork. I write little blurbs here and product descriptions there. I create web page text now and even write wedding vows, which of course flow naturally from me given my background writing romance. I freelance through Upwork, Fiverr, Guru, People Per Hour, Toptal, FlexJobs, 99designs…you name it! I could really use an assistant to help me keep track of all my deadlines nowadays! Know anyone good? Oh, just kidding, Jill." Mary teased her. "I know you must have better things to do with your time."

"You know, you really did inspire me to become a writer, Mary. I thought 'Taken By Storm' was so taboo at the time. I used to hide that copy you signed for me under my mattress every night like it was an issue of Hustler magazine or something. I really took to it! That was the same summer I kissed a boy for the first time too, and right on the nose!"

"I remember!" Mary said. "I still have that story you emailed me from college. What was the name of that one again? Was it 'No Experience Necessary?'" Mary made an educated guess while Jill racked her brain trying to remember the title of her own story.

"No, I think it was 'Before Boys, There Was Candy,'" Jill finally remembered.

"Oh yes! That was it! How could I forget? I always thought that would be a brilliant title for your debut novel!"

"Thanks." Jill took the compliment like a dagger to the heart because she knew that she would never finish writing that debut novel.

Before she knew it, her mind was playing tricks on her again. *Jill, your mentor is really nothing more than a one-hit-wonder. She is never going to finish that sequel to Taken By Storm that she has been promising her fans ever since you were a kid.*

"Have you published yet?" Mary flipped the script on her protegé faster than a looming deadline.

Jill knew that was a yes or no question but instead, she beat around the bush about it, overthinking her answer, antsy and anxious as she spontaneously rose to her feet to pace the length of her lover's condo while staring down at the scattered piles of notebook paper she left on the floor

A bunch of half baked ideas written in my own chicken scratch, that do not amount to a hill of beans.

"Oh...you know, I still dabble." Jill caught Dream out of the corner of her eye, swatting at another crumpled-up piece of paper with writing on it. "I've been batting around a few ideas lately. I really should get organized. Get a writing coach. Do something!" Jill knew she sounded frustrated with herself and tried to tone the self-loathing down a bit. "I have to be inspired to write again I guess. The time for old projects has passed. I guess I let those opportunities slip through my fingers like everything else that has slipped through the cracks in my life. It has all been wasted time."

She trailed off, rubbing the back of her neck red with her dominant hand, without knowing she was doing it, as if the appendage had somehow taken on a life of its own, beating with the pulse of a Tell-Tale Heart that was only getting louder.

"I guess I was just out of the loop until the pandemic hit and I moved back to the big city."

"You moved back to the city? Well, that is great news! What have you been doing since you got there?" Mary inquired with interest.

Jill was too embarrassed to answer that question honestly, so she did not respond.

"Are you writing again?" Mary asked bluntly.

"No. I am not…listen, Mary, I really don't want to talk about it… okay? Can we just change the subject, please?" Jill could feel her forehead breaking out into itchy oozing hives, like small painful mosquito bites that appeared from out of nowhere."

"You should have called me! I still have clients in Chicago, you know? In fact, I have something you can do for me…"

"What is it?" Jill asked suspiciously but Mary was already off to the races, actively engaged in the one activity she excelled at in life which was letting other people do her work for her.

"This is the perfect gig for you, Jill. Actually, it's more like two gigs rolled into one for the price of three, isn't that exciting?"

"Oh, uhu," Jill stated flatly, sounding not at all convinced. "I thought you were the kind of writer who never turned down work Mary?"

"Well, that might be true but I guess I thought these gigs could help you get your creative juices flowing again since it sounds like you are stuck in a rut! We must continually be challenging ourselves as artists, you know. Say… by the way, which pseudonym are you using these days? I should pass that info along to my clients so they do not get confused when they work with you."

"G.G. Maxwell," Jill said, "and I haven't said yes or agreed to do anything..."

"Yet." Mary finished Jill's sentence before asking, "What do those initials stand for anyways? G.G.? I mean, what is that? Some sort of play on E.E. Cummings name?"

"What? No, those were E.E. 's actual initials. G.G. is an example of initialism itself. It stands for Greatest Ghostwriter."

"Oh, interesting. Well, now you can start living up to your pseudonym and I think this is the perfect place to start, with these clients," Mary declared. "I am really excited about this opportunity I am giving you! Let me just dive right in and tell you a little more about these fascinating clients.

Darling is a comedian, also a character actor. From the UK. She is trying to make a comeback as a middle-aged comedian. She used to perform a lot in her 20s, so she is familiar with all that jazz that goes along with being a stage performer. Let's see...what else? Oh yeah, this woman wears wigs, designer dresses, and

bobbles and fringe. She is actually quite fancy. She reminds me of that mother from Schitt's Creek who used to be high society like in her former life. You know the one...that washed-up middle-aged actress who nails all her wigs to the walls in that dreadfully cheap motel? Darling's act should be a breeze for you to write because you can relate to her. She just turned 50 too."

"I am not 50, Mary! My birthday is still months away," Jill snapped.

"Oh relax! I stand corrected." Mary blew off the comment as Jill flipped her the bird behind the camera on her phone. "All I meant by it is that you should be able to relate to her because you are both single and going through... Well, you know, THE CHANGE."

"Oh, uhu." Jill just kept repeating her favorite canned response.

"The second client I am sending your way is Soda Pop Pink."

"What the hell is THAT?" Jill asked.

"Their pronouns are—" Mary began to explain..

"Whoa, whoa, wait a minute. Hold up. I do not write for people who are going to insist on me using their pronouns. It's too fucking weird and complicated and I just can't relate to that zoomer garbage."

"Now, hold up, wait a minute," Mary countered, "Just hear me out for once. I know that taking someone young on as a client is a bit of a challenge because she is new to the comedy world hails from a different generation. But I think if anyone can pull this off, you can, Jill. I really do! And I am sure you could use the income coming in."

"Well, at least her pronoun is she, that is one thing we have in common."

"See!"

"How young is SHE?"

"Oh, you know Gen Z-ish," Mary remained vague in her description of this character.

"Mary, that is a generation not an age, How old is she exactly?"

"Barely legal, 19."

"19? Really? Mary, where the hell do you find these clients?"

"Well, typically online. But Soda Pop Pink is actually a very successful social media influencer. My glam babies follow her on TikTok.

"What is a glam baby?"

"Just a fun word for grandkids. Do you have a TikTok account?"

"Ummmm, that is a negative."

"Well, this TikTok influencer has millions of followers."

"Oh really? And why should I care?" Jill rolled her eyes up in the air. "Okay, that is a fair question… Why should you care?"

"Exactly! You know they/them speak a language all their own. They basically speak in code and their hair makes me want to puke Skittles."

"LMFAO!" Mary said. "There you go making me laugh out loud again. You see? You have half the material to write an act already. You truly are a natural, Jill! Truly funny as hell."

"Yeah, but ragging on Zoomers? That sounds more like something Darling would do, not Soda Pop Pink." Jill corrected her mentor.

"You see? You are already starting to flesh out the characters and make them more three dimensional, creating the show as you go along. Writing two shows in your head at the same time! Hell, the shows are writing themselves. Can't you see? You have got this in the bag kid. I have faith in you and so I am going to go ahead and give them your phone number and have them…"

"No Mary, email only. I insist."

"Okay…email it will be! I am so glad you have decided to get back into the swing of things. I really do need to point out that these performances run back to back, at different clubs, on the same night, one week from Saturday. So please make sure you check your emails often and start writing as soon as the clients pay you for the gigs so you can finish writing them on time. Do you have an online bank account? I will have them pass on their information.

I am going to bat for you on this Jill, because I think you are a brilliant writer and a great friend. Consider yourself fully vetted by me, sincerely Mary Gold!" Mary Gold said.

"Wait!" Jill insisted. "First, I want to know why you are passing these clients over if this is such a stellar opportunity and one of the gigs pays double. I mean, did you win the lottery or something? What is really going on here? What is the catch? Why are you trying to clear your calendar? You had better spill the tea this instant!"

"OK, but promise me you won't tell a soul… Promise!" Mary insisted.

"Like who the hell would I tell, Mary? We don't even know the same people."

"Good point. Anyways, Roman is coming to visit on Saturday and he is staying for three days because my ex husband takes the kids every other weekend." Mary sounded over the moon.

"Who is this Roman character, anyways?" Jill asked.

"We met on IG"

"You mean THAT scammer?"

"Actually, he is not scamming me at all. You see, we have a real connection, Jill. I am telling you! Anyway, he works on an oil rig way out in the middle of the ocean."

"Which ocean?"

"I don't know for crying out loud, it may be a sea. Anyways, that part is not important. The point is that I gave Roman my address to ship some of his baggage over in advance of his flight here to meet me because…"

"Wait a minute…What the fuck?" Jill did not even allow her

mentor to finish her explanation before she muted the RHOA to talk some sense into Mary. "What in the actual fuck are you thinking. Are you for real? I mean, you do not know this man from Adam."

"Roman!" Mary snapped back. "I told you his name is Roman!"

"Okay, perfect! Because *that* name does not sound totally made the fuck up like a character out of one of your non existent romance novels. I mean, come on, you write fiction so I know, for a fact, that you don't care about the truth Mary! And besides, you have no idea what kind of illegal merchandise this scammer is trying to smuggle into America. And you still have young ones at home! Haven't you ever watched the show *Locked Up Abroad*? I mean, what is the first thing they ask you at the airport when you wheel your bags through customs, for Christ's sake, Mary? I mean, COME ON!"

"Okay, look. I do appreciate your concern, I really do, but I am an adult and older than you. I can make my own decisions and I do have a real connection with Roman. Our love is like nothing I have never experienced before! We sing to each other on the phone. He takes virtual walks with me. Well, I am walking and he is virtual. He even invited me to his daughter's birthday next month in Italy! I sent her a gift card."

"Repeat after me Mary... 'No nudes, no money, no baggage.' And I want you to make this your mantra from now on. Do not send him any nude photos or videos of yourself. Do not give him any money or accept anything from him in the mail, no letters, no baggage."

"But I haven't!"

"Yes you have. Didn't you just get finished telling me that you sent his daughter a gift card for her birthday?"

"Yeah but to her, not to him. Well, to a PO box, I guess,

because she is between addresses.

"That sounds about right. Listen, Mary, I really need to go. I will keep an eye out for those emails and let you know how the clients work out, okay? It was great catching up. Now repeat after me... No nudes, no money, no baggage."

"Yeah, yeah...You are no fun anymore, you know that?"

"Well, I do aim to please." Jill smiled with a fed-up grin before logging off.

"Later Gator," Mary added, "Peace out." She threw up two fingers.

The following day Jill was back to binge-watching the Real Housewives of every major city on earth. She spent most of her afternoon on the couch watching all the characters' dreams come true because somebody paid them to make that happen when suddenly her cell sent out a notification that she had received emails from both Darling and Soda Pop Pink at the same time. Each was inquiring about her services and so Jill responded to them briefly by describing herself and requesting payment for the writing services that she offered up front.

After they transferred money into her online account Jill knew she still had almost a week to write comedy for them and so she continued to watch Housewives, telling herself as each episode ended that she was only going to catch one more episode before she started writing. But after several days flew by, she was in too deep—and then she had to catch the season finale because she knew somebody was going to get the smackdown.

Before she noticed it Friday night had crept up on her and she was scrambling to meet her Saturday writing deadline in full panic mode. Clearly, she had not planned ahead, nor had she heeded her mentor's warning to start writing as soon as her clients paid. So now she had only four hours left to write stand-up for both shows as they were being performed back-to-back.

She decided to focus on Soda Pop Pink's material first because she knew that Gen Z spoke a language all their own, so that meant it would take more time to make this material sound believable so it would likely take longer to write. Jill also wanted to put the most effort into this show because this client had paid double and Jill knew if she focused she could provide this social media sensation with funny and valuable content that was relevant to her generation. Something that would keep her followers coming back for more.

Jill wrote this first monologue in a language that any zoomer could understand, given that the 'comedian' performing it was barely an adult herself.

And who knows? Soda Pop may choose to get drunk and high during her show and just want to party with her fans instead of actually finishing the set because, you know how shit goes bro!

THE EARLY SHOW

PROPS NEEDED:

One manual pump super soaker filled with water.

THE MONOLOGUE:

"SUH!!!! Vibe check one two one two?

Locked down in the middle of a pandemic with no sauce, becoming a drip because, no pregame. Can't hang with my homies, no situationship, low body count.

Stuck inside with the FAM but I want to slam, so not hot. They wanna go glamping. I want them to say less or somebody is bound to catch hands, big yikes!

I missed out on some serious smash, spring break and graduation due to cancel culture and now the government wants to snatch up my lady rights? So my vibe is that Mercury is in retrograde and I am starting to feel like bitter is my new bestie,"

"Okurrr!!!!!!" The comedian belts out the word Cardi B made famous before the K clan stole it.

"I am not trying to get pregnant either because you know how that shit goes ladies. Let's just say the quiet part out loud… Are you ready? Here we go!"

"No Roe, No Hoe!" The comedian shouts as she pumps her fist in the air. "Repeat after me ladies!"

The comedian points the microphone at the women in the audience encouraging them to repeat the same phrase

"No Roe, No Hoe!"

The comedian continues this back and forth motion with the mic until she gets all the ladies so fired up that they are pumping their fists high as a kite as they continue to chant the slogan.

The comedian takes a beat then playfully seduces the guys in the audience by licking the microphone as she spreads her legs seductively.

"But before I close my legs for the last time, I want to squirt all you snacks out there with my super soaker!"

The comedian cries out as she grabs the prop gun, primes the pump super slow, like she is jacking off a dick, and then aims it at all the thirsty males standing in the front row.

"Time to cool off bros!" The comedian hoses them down without missing a beat.

"Besides, virtual is where it's at now, not IRL. In fact, I think I fall in love virtually every time you comment on my social media content." The comedian blows virtual kisses to the guys before blowing on the end of that super soaker as if it were a smoking gun before she struts off stage real slow with the super soaker dangling from that flashy holster attached to her hip.

It was only after Jill had drafted both acts that she realized she really had no idea whatsoever how much material her clients even required to perform an entire show.

She had never bothered to ask how long their bits needed to be so she just fudged the length of the material, throwing in a few extra jokes and props for good measure, just in case the jokes bombed and the clients happened to be skilled at physical comedy like some kind of Lucille Ball type character.

After emailing each client their respective material, moments before the deadline, Jill crashed face-down in her lover's bed, next to an ashtray filled with a mound of smoldering cigarettes and a few rolled joints that she had never lit the night before because she was far too nervous to inhale the smoke from them for long enough to get high.

It was late afternoon before Jill fell out of bed after having way overslept the alarm clock that she never set for herself. She had no idea how long she had been passed out but she had to hurry up and get dressed due to the fact that she was already running late for the early show.

When Jill arrived outside Calamities comedy club she instantly recognized her TikTok client from the many viral videos the influencer had posted online. She was the tall blonde that was taking to the stage, donning a powder pink space suit and thigh-high stripper boots that glittered like gold in the setting sun. She was not wearing a holster but she was certainly fun to look at if nothing else.

She was rocking that 'I dream of Genie' blonde bombshell partial updo, with her golden locks tied in a twisted top knot that dangled halfway down her back thicker than any Mane 'n Tail that God had ever created for one of his creatures, much like some futuristic space fantasy pin up type of pop star.

Jill had taken her place, standing on the sidelines like a professional wallflower as she began to study the face of the character that she had helped to create. It was then that she noticed that there was no super soaker on stage and the show was about to begin. She watched as Soda Pop Pink scrolled through her iPhone as if she was about to do a cold read of the material Jill had written for her without rehearsing her lines.

"What do celebrities and women in menopause have in common?" Soda Pop Pink asked her audience. They seemed confused by the question.

"They all wanna fuck their fans!" She began fondling the fan that had been placed on the stage, in front of her, to keep the talent cool in that intense August heat. And the air was so thick that you could cut it with a knife thanks to the fact that nobody seemed amused by the joke or understood the punch line.

Jill slipped out the back door to hop the L train back to the Gold Coast before the shit hit the fan. She could not believe that she had mixed up the jokes she wrote for Darling with the material that was now being performed, *live on stage*, by Soda Pop Pink!

THE DEVIL ON HER SHOULDER

Jill was far too preoccupied with her problems to notice that she had just boarded a train that was bound straight for hell, as the heavy metal jaws of the L swung wide open to swallow up all the people on the platform.

It was during this time that the devil appeared. It had blown in with the wind, much like all the other trash in the city, to plop itself down on her shoulder, right on top of the weight of the world which was already there, in order to whisper awful things into her ear, in a low and menacing tone of voice that only she could hear.

The devil came to school her on the modals of lost opportunities that she had blown off, also known as the could have, would have, and should have game and the devil always made the first move.

"You could have double-checked those email addresses before you sent that material to the wrong clients and then everything would have been okay. What the fuck is wrong with you? You really are worthless, you know that?" The devil berated her.

"You should have taken Mary's advice and started writing those monologues as soon as you got paid and then you would not have panicked and fucked things up so bad but you simply could not get your act together in time, could you? You are completely unprofessional. You have never been prepared to complete any of the work you set out to do, no matter how simple the assignment, how much you get paid, or how much time you have to get the work done. Nobody is ever going to take you seriously as a writer and you will never work in this town again.

You could still warn Darling about that monologue mix-up before it's too late so why haven't you? What are you waiting for? I thought comedy writers understood the value of timing? What a joke! Your career is just like that sequel that Mary will never write, *Taken By Storm*, because she is an impostor just like you. The same as Truman Capote. You are all the same, never living up to your true potential.

So utterly out of touch with reality that you have created this rich facade to hide behind as if every day were a black and white ball where you can hide behind a mask. You are never going to have a career in comedy and your lover will soon grow tired of

saving the day for you when you are clearly not capable of saving yourself from being forever rescued.

"Didn't you read Great Expectations? You were warned about the other woman a long time ago. The one that gets passed over and thrown away. But I guess you weren't paying attention in English Literature that day? Daydreaming again, I suppose. You really ARE a fucking fool!

"Are you going to be the rejected one? The one that was left behind? Playing second fiddle to his teenage wet dream…some Hooters waitress who seduced him in a half shirt before she landed the cover of Maxim for obvious reasons?

Well? Are you? Answer me, damn it! The clock is ticking and your life is halfway over! Are you going to spend the rest of it rotting away in this prison of your own making, forced to relive the day you met him over and over again all because you can't find a life to move on with? Because if that is the case, my job is finished here and I can finally wash my hands of you and find someone else to torture because you are pretty much stuck on stupid for the rest of your life.

Jill tried her best to ignore the devil but the insults were coming at her rapid-fire and she could not stop herself from overthinking every mistake that she had ever made in her entire life and that included Max.

"You are, perhaps, even more delusional than Miss Havisham was, after all," The devil continued. "An even more tragic sort of spinster type figure altogether. Hell, at least that crazy old bitch GOT a proposal. Max never proposed to you. Maybe try chewing on that instead of all that deep dish pizza you keep shoveling into your pie hole, washing it down with all the lies he has been feeding you, consuming his bullshit. You only get one shot at this life Jill and your time is running out, TikTok, TikTok!"

The devil continued to lambaste her as the train rolled into the next station, where it slowed to a crawl. Jill was peering out of the window when she spotted a man who was kneeling in the melting heart yoga position on the platform. His head was bowed as if he were a praying mantis in deep meditation. His limbs were long and lean. In his hands he held a red solo cup raised over his lowered head. He appeared to be begging for change without making a sound and in the most passive way possible.

"Meekness is not weakness," Jill kept repeating this wisdom in her head as a way of comforting herself as she rocked back and forth with the motion of the L in an effort to control her growing anxiety.

"You do understand that you are only one paycheck away from being THAT beggar? You know your 'lover' is not going to let you live in his kingdom forever, right?"

No longer in control, Jill felt the tears streaming down her cheeks.

"You have no game, Jill, so now it is time for me to take over again because you would rather cry your eyes out than learn to play ball and fall in line like the rest of the team.

You have no crumb of knowledge about what it actually means to be homeless but you think you can relate? Or is it just that you are feeling sorry for yourself again? Because the reality is that you can no longer take care of yourself. You will never be able to support yourself as an artist. You will always be at the mercy of lovers and strangers who cover all of your living expenses so that you do not have to face getting a real job or perform any unspeakable acts in order to cover the rent. But what happens when he cuts you off? He isn't going to let you live like this, rent-free, forever. And nobody wants a dried-up old fifty-year-old hag. He is playing the field like the rest of them because he knows that he can.

I know exactly how this story will end and I must say that it gives me great pleasure to give you a glimpse into your own fucked up future," said the devil, who now appeared to be channeling Ebenezer Scrooge in its latest attempt to make Jill's life a living hell.

The doors of the L blew wide open and the chilly autumn air crept in while the sun set low behind the bruised clouds, scattered low across the late summer sky.

"The first thing that is going to happen when he throws you out is that you will lose your mind because that is always the first thing to go when you run out of money to pay for your many vices that help you to forget about your past.

Then you are going to spiral out of control when your night terrors return because you cannot afford weed. Naturally, I will be making a guest star appearance in those mind altering experiences."

Jill began to rummage through her brand-new Telfar handbag, the one she had just purchased in purple because she loved how vibrant the color of it was and because she saw Sasha Tara carrying that same bag in the latest magazine spreads.

She was desperately searching for the receipt so that she could use it to return the purse along with all the other high-dollar purchases she had made as of late, with those advances she got for writing the comedy she screwed up.

Suddenly her cell phone started chirping. An unknown number flashed across the screen on her caller ID. She did not want to answer it, in case it was a client. She turned the ringer off.

"What the fuck do you think you are doing? You should have answered that call! What if it was Darling? What if it was Soda Pop asking for her money back after you already spent it? You are going to really piss off Soda who may pop off if you ignore her calls after you fucked up her show.

She could totally trash you out on social media. And you cannot afford to piss off Darling either! Then both of them are going to be after you to pay them back and I bet you they won't waste any time asking for refunds either.

What if they try to sue you for defamation? Oh no, wait a minute, I forgot, they can't do that because there is nothing to take from you, because YOU are broke as a joke. Get it? You have nothing."

Jill waited to see if the mystery caller would leave a voicemail but they did not.

The devil laughed hysterically, as Jill realized it was drawing closer and closer to the time Darling was due to perform her act in a comedy club that was half way across town.

Jill's hand was trembling as she searched for the original email Darling had sent her to inquire about her services, so she could send her an apology for sending her the wrong material and make things right prior to her performance.

When Jill could not locate the email, her heart started to

pound faster and faster until it felt like it was about to explode right out of her chest. She knew she was having a panic attack because she was gasping for air and her mask was collapsing in on her face so she ripped it off.

She took a long deep breath in with her eyes closed, then opened them up to see several other passengers were riding the train without their masks on either.

Jill's hypochondria launched her straight back into panic mode as she was now convinced that she had inhaled their shared air so she must have caught Covid from them when they coughed. Jill hated her hypochondria and she was beginning to wonder if this condition that she suffered from was just another way for the devil to play games with her in order to live rent-free in her head.

Jill stood up and moved to a private area at the back of the train where two seats faced in the opposite direction of the way in which the train was traveling.

There, she sat alone, trying to engage in some belly breathing to calm her nerves, as she frantically searched for that original email from Darling which she eventually found sitting in her spam folder alongside the original email she received from Soda Pop Pink.

She started composing several drafts of an apology letter to Darling but she could not bring herself to send any of them as she was too busy freaking out about catching Covid from the other strangers on the train to remain focused.

So finally she just gave up altogether, saved the last draft she had composed, closed her eyes, popped in her earbuds to listen to music and drown out the devil, as she slid down low on the unforgiving metal seat to find a more laid back position which made her feel invisible.

Before long, she fell fast asleep. She missed her stop

completely and then had to ride the train all the way to the end of the line, and backtrack for miles, in a cab with a driver who also refused to wear a mask.

When she returned to her lover's condo, clear on the other side of the city, she spent a restless night drinking and smoking as she listened to the heavy raindrops beating down on the floor-to-ceiling windows with an intensity that matched her sullen mood.

"WAKE THE FUCK UP!"

The devil screamed in stereo, causing Jill to sit straight up as it pulled the weight of its red-hot body across her back to slither up her spine, like a snake, as it crawled over the curve on her tensed shoulder.

"You have wasted most of your life sssssleeping," The devil hissed in a slow and steady tone as it intermittently injected its bifurcated tongue into her waxy ear hole.

"How can you sssstill be so tired? All you do is lay around and fucking sssssleep? Are you sssssick? You are sssick, sssick in the head. Not strong enough to control your vicccces or this voiccce so I guess I will continue to haunt you just like this, just like those freaky twins from the *Shining* who Danny saw. Forever, and ever, until the day you realize that life was never meant to be fun and games for a fool like you. How many things have you put off doing since you came to Chicago? How much time have you squandered you lazy bitch? How many opportunities have you missed?" The devil hissed.

"I am so fed up with all your fucking excuses. Time waits for no one. A million have died from the pandemic, but believe me, the band marches on. And even after all the death and destruction, if you even survive it all, you will never come out on the other side of this thing with your sanity intact. Maybe you will be more mentally ill than ever. Maybe you will be so paralyzed by fear that it renders you incapable of making decisions for yourself

and then you will become a ward of the state. They will put you in a group home.

Do you really want to continue to drink, smoke, and screw your way out of happiness, suffering every misfortune you are forced to endure until the day you die?

You should not be getting high. You should be preparing yourself for the next great disaster in your life because this one is going to hit you like a freight train soon so you should be scared shitless about that because you have no plan and your life will soon spiral out of control and to make matters worse, you have become a burden on every person who has ever loved you and soon there will be no one left to care for you and you will be left alone to wallow in your pain in some random group home.

The knights in shining armor are half your age now and they have no interest in rescuing spinsters in menopause.

The only flowers you will receive, from this day forward, will be the cheap carnation and chrysanthemums carelessly thrown at your grave by a groundskeeper who happens to pity the dead and long ago forgotten.

Sirens began to sound off in the city as Jill clutched her throat, in panic mode, wondering if the dry lump that had formed there was due to anxiety, fear, or if she had finally caught Covid.

At the same time, she could feel a hot flash coming on and it was all-consuming this time around. So she raced to the bathroom where she took the coldest shower she could stand before retiring to the bedroom to sleep on her stomach with her wet back and fat bottom pointed straight up at the ceiling fan, which was racing at a fever pitch.

She was wondering if Max really did have cameras installed

in the bedroom to watch her as she slept naked and masturbated in his bed, a fantasy the devil immediately squashed.

"So many distractions, so little time," the devil taunted Jill. "You can't handle a regular job like neurotypical people do but you live in a capitalist society so basically no one is ever going to value you as a person because you have nothing to bring to the table. Society will always judge you, always see you as 'less than' and nothing more than a worthless feeder, you know, and better off as fodder for the worms."

Jill was too exhausted to fight back, so she just lay there listening to the devil scream into her ear until she finally passed out.

It was not long at all before the devil came to call on her again, only now it was daylight out and Jill caught a glimpse of her own reflection in her lover's over-sized vanity.

"You look like some sort of nasty ass wooly beast with your hairy legs, stained nightshirt, and sad hanging sacks for tits." The devil said.

"Gaining weight again? Eating in your lover's bed again, I see. You androgynous fatty fuck! He told you that you look better with makeup than without but you don't wear makeup anymore and still you expect to live up to his great expectations? He never considered you a natural beauty. He always told you that you looked better in makeup.

Do you honestly think you are the only one? Too much of a fucking coward to ask him about it because you can't handle the truth? Hell, for all you know, he could have married that Maxim model he met at Hooters.

He says he can't visit you due to the pandemic, too risky to fly his private plane. This is a red flag, Jill because he has family in this state.

He does not love you, he only pities you, so he is throwing money at your problem until you are gone. You really mean very little to him, and the money means even less because he has so much of it to spare.

You are his spare, his just in case girl or maybe not even that."

Jill pulled the covers over her head and turned her back on the vanity to curl up in a ball where she cried herself back to sleep.

She woke up sometime later with her head down at the foot of the bed, tangled up in satin sheets as if she were bound by BTK when suddenly she caught a whiff of something that really stank.

She moved her head whilst staying in the same prone position to peer over the edge of the mattress that she had just finished drooling on and over yonder she spotted this sea of dirty laundry that she had neglected to wash since the day she soiled it because she was too busy battling the devil to get anything done.

"You can't win, Jill, I have been with you since childhood because you let me in. You alone are responsible. All of this is your fault.

Those intense hot flashes you are experiencing that are completely out of control? They make you want to punch someone in the fucking face. Those hot flashes that make you feel like you want to cause pain because you are out of your mind?

Nothing to see here. Just another middle-aged loser with a bad haircut and a shitty attitude. You can't control your rage, and you're incapable of taking care of yourself. This is when the real nightmares begin for you because you won't be able to afford the weed you need to smoke to keep the monster at bay and you will be far too terrified to sleep at night on top of those uncontrollable hot flashes you have that make you agitated and extra angry.

What is going to happen when you lose control? A middle-aged starving artist with hot flashes and a bad haircut who suffers from anxiety and depression, not right in the mind, living in a city with a bunch of other people who are not in their right minds either. You cut your hair off so you are no longer attractive and you cannot take care of yourself because you are sick in the head."

You can no longer take care of yourself, loser!

Jill cried herself back to sleep as the devil talked in circles around her.

TEN POUND GORILLA

It was a loud rapping at the door, only that and nothing more, that stirred Jill from sleep.

Her mother knocked that way, loud as hell, with a complete sense of urgency, even though there was never an emergency. She had even busted a window out that way once, when she had come to call one afternoon in order to bring her daughter soup.

Jill was sick and upstairs sleeping, and her mother got so pissed off for being unheard and feeling ignored that she punched a hole straight through the one-of-a-kind stained glass windows she'd just had custom installed in the front door.

Of course, she blamed the entire incident on the wind as she blew through the place like a tornado on fire, expelling shards of colored glass in her wake, leaving Jill to clean up the broken pieces of the rainbow long after the diva peeled out of the front yard in her red hot Fahrvergnugen, backing out over the devil strip and leaving her own newly seeded lawn in a muddled mess of total disarray.

If Jill had been carrying a monkey around in her purse, thought, her mother must have been lugging around a ten-pound gorilla in that oversized European carryall she dragged around.

This notion made her smile, a little, for once, as she found herself laughing at the cleverness of her own ripe
 imagination.

Wait, what if Max was knocking at the door? Surely, he must have a key to his own castle, but what if he had come to surprise her?

It was this idea that made her heart skip a beat, giving her a sudden burst of energy. It made her so spry that she flipped right out of the bed, like a ninja on steroids, landing with both feet planted firmly on the floor, where she dusted another layer of crusty crumbs off her curves before digging her stubby, flaking painted black nails deep into her frizzy hair, to shake it out like Ally Sheedy from *The Breakfast Club*.

Quickly, she raced off to the bathroom to grab the stool she used to take a proper dump with, so she could raise her own shorty ass up high enough to peer through the peephole, to see who was at the door.

She was confused as to find Shantay standing outside. Shantay was her favorite door person, but she only worked on Wednesdays.

Jill was convinced it was still Saturday because yesterday was the day that she had fucked up her whole life and thrown her career away.

She kicked the stool aside and slowly opened the door without removing the chain. Shantay stood before Jill wearing a sharp, gray, tailored, charcoal pinstriped suit and a pair of Mary Jane shoes. There were so many things Jill wanted to say to her but she could not express herself through that sliver in the door that divided the inside world from the outside world. She tried to speak but to no avail. Instead, she found herself simply standing there, staring at the surprise visitor who had come to call.

"Unlock this door," Shantay insisted.

Jill immediately slid the chain off the latch. She then stood there trying to act all nonchalant, as she clutched at the collar of the crusty towel she had just thrown on over the stained Batman onesie she had just peeled off the floor, and slipped into, before answering the door.

"Why is it so dark and spooky and smells so dank in this place? It ain't Halloween!" Shantay furrowed her brow at the sight and smell of Jill as she proceeded to give her the once over. "Ummmm, hello? You don't call, you don't write, you don't go out. You know what you are? You the Human Stain." She raised one eyebrow, slightly higher than the famous cross dresser Divine, in order to put a finer point on the shade she was throwing at Jill as she snickered to herself softly.

"Excuse me, what was that last part? Did you say... The Human Stain? Oh, I loved that movie! You must be a huge fan of drama?" Jill tried nervously to relate to this statuesque Nubian queen who was now looming large over the troubled tenant as she stood in front of Jill eating a bag of chips.

"Child, please. I was serious about that human stain part. That get-up you got on, that you been ghosting around here in, is not cute. In fact, it is crusty AF. How come I always see you wearing the same damn thing? You trying to appear homeless? Were you a squatter?"

"No..."

"Didn't I show you where the laundry room is? I thought I gave you the grand tour on the day you moved in."

"You did but I forgot how to get there."

Shantay shook down the bag of Doritos she was gripping in her long claws like she was shaking down the latest daddy she expected to Remy up for the new set of acrylics she had to have. "So, why are you ghosting? Nobody seen you downstairs in days so this here is your wellness check."

Shantay spun the pointer finger on her free hand down and around in a hypnotic spiraling motion as she pointed to the spot where Jill was standing.

Jill could not speak and so she just stared blankly up at the door woman who was fishing around inside that bag of chips she was holding before she surgically removed a sliver of crisp from it with an impressive tweezers like grip of her fingertips as if she had been a child playing a precision game of Operation. She then held that orange sliver of that golden triangle up to the light to inspect it. She was holding it so close to her face that she nearly went cross eyed.

"So, what day is it, girl?" Shantay suddenly snapped out of her trance to focus her attention on Jill as she stared daggers into her eyes to begin her interrogation.

"Saturday? No, wait, no... Sunday?" Jill kept guessing.

"Okay, is that your final answer?" Shantay smacked her lips together, in a way that made it abundantly clear to Jill that
she was no match for this city slicker who was clearly concerned with her complete lack of awareness since it did appear
that Jill had no clue what was going on.

"Yes?" Jill was acting like a contestant on Jeopardy, as she carefully responded to each question with an answer in the form of a question.

"Wow!" Shantay shook her head back and forth, to indicate that she was disappointed as she proceeded to nibble on the edge of that impossibly small sliver of corn chip she had pinched off, chewing each bite super slow as if she had a right to take her good old time doing whatever she damn well pleased.

Jill was mesmerized by the audio and visual elements of this ASMR experience that was unfolding before her, what with all the clicking and clacking of the fingernails and the crinkling and crunching sounds that Shantay was making with that bag of chips.

Maybe this is how Shantay manages to maintain her slim figure. She just chews on the same damn chip all day long. I mean, how many calories could that possibly be? I bet she mesmerizes every man she meets by eating chips that way. And I bet she does not take any bullshit from any of their dumb asses either!

"Okay, so, you do not know what day it is, duly noted." Shantay interrupted Jill's daydreaming as she dipped her fingertips back into that bag of chips to remove another sliver.

Jill could tell that Shantay was making mental notes of everything she told her, probably so she could use it against her later in a 51/50 scenario if it ever came to blows and the cops got called.

"Okay, what time is it?" Shantay asked.

"Look, I don't really know right now because I may have misplaced my phone," Jill mumbled.

"May have?" Shantay quipped.

"Look, I don't really know, okay? I thought I had it yesterday."

"Yesterday?"

"Yes, yesterday. Why? Do you need to know what time it is?" Jill turned around as if she was about to wander off to search for her cell phone when suddenly she began to feel faint and so she leaned up against the door frame to support herself instead.

"No, *you* need to know what time it is!" Shantay raised her forearm up sideways, in slow motion, in order to reveal the bold face of the new Rolex watch she was wearing.

"Oh Damn!" Jill exclaimed. "You know, you kind of remind me of Duckie Thot, the South Sudanese Australian model, for some reason, I feel like I am experiencing deja vu right now, for real. Like I saw this play out in a dream somewhere.

I was having this vision about how you just landed some lucrative contract with Rolex, that requires you to launch their latest watches while posing effortlessly for Pirelli, the famous calendar, along with an all-black cast of other models. Is that thing really real?"

"What the watch? More real than déjà vu, child. Do you even know what that even means?"

"Yeah...like something you feel like you have experienced before."

"No." Shantay corrected her. It is actually just a miscommunication of the brain, like the one you are currently experiencing."

"Oh really? Is that so?"

"So, just for the record..." Shantay continued to make mental notes out loud. "Does not know what day or time it is, lost her phone, and possibly her damn mind." Shantay counted on her fingers as she continued to gather details about Jill as if she was the subject of interrogation that she was not actually present.

"Look! I am certain it is somewhere here, lying dead under a pile of clothes. It's just a matter of time before I find it, okay? I mean, I did not start drinking until AFTER I got home from the show last night, so..."

"Last night?" Shantay corrected Jill. "Oh no child. You been passed out for days. This here is Wednesday." Shantay pointed down to the place where Jill was standing in the door frame, in order to drive home the point that Jill was actually present in that moment.

"Look! I am okay, really! I mean, Who is asking anyways? Did someone call the front desk to check in on me? Was it Max?" Jill was becoming increasingly agitated and paranoid as she clutched at the bath towel she was wearing over his dirty laundry.

She spontaneously lunged forward, causing Shantay to take one giant leap back, in order to allow Jill to pop her head out into the hallway, to ensure that they were there alone.

"Paranoid much?" Shantay asked. What have you been smoking? That is rank." She started swatting at invisible flies near her nose once she caught a whiff of the weed that was wafting through the stale air.

"Look, I swear on my mother's grave *and* the bible that I am perfectly fine. I just want to know who is asking? That's all."
Jill insisted.

"Is your mother really dead? You need to stop playing with me" Shantay insisted.

"No! But, she is dead to me!" Jill shocked the shit out of herself
when those words flew straight out of her mouth as if she was finally giving a voice to the way she felt all along.

"Look, you are acting kind of irrational so I am going to order you something to eat and bring it up here when it gets delivered and until then, please stay inside, okay?"

"Oh, thanks but no thanks!" Jill declined the offer as she began to back away from the open door. "I couldn't eat right now! I am on a diet. Besides, I can always walk down to the 7/11 and grab a bite later, if I get hungry."

"So... that was not you who ordered food for this unit yesterday? I saw the delivery on the security camera. You didn't order a deep dish with a two liter bottle of diet cherry coke and a slice of Tiramisu from Giordanos?" Or did you feed all that to your cat?"

"I don't even remember eating any of it!" Jill trailed off because she was ashamed of herself.

"Listen, you need to eat something today, and before you pass out, that's all I am saying. This does not need to be a big production. Find and charge your phone and I will call you up after they deliver the food, okay? So just sit tight. I'll be back to check up on you in about an hour, alright? Do you want a side salad with your meal?"

"No, I fucking hate salad!" Jill snapped before they parted ways.

Jill found her cell phone lying sideways behind the toilet, where she had dropped it last, apparently days prior. She plugged it in before collapsing in a puddle of tears on the floor, behind that massive condo door, famished and confused.

"Shantay really is all that *and* a bag of chips." Jill tried to focus on having positive thoughts to avoid experiencing another visit from the devil.

By the time Shantay delivered her pizza, Jill was so hungry that she practically inhaled the entire thing before passing out on the couch right in front of her new house guest, who simply seemed to overlook all her rude behavior.

When Jill woke up next, she was lying on her back with her neck twisted sideways on the couch. Her bloated belly was sticking straight up in the air and one of her legs was dragging on the floor when her cell phone rang out of the clear blue sky.

"Damn! You gonna answer that call?" Shantay, hovered over Jill on the couch as she held the ringing phone.

Jill grabbed her cell to answer the restricted call. "Hello?" She said. She was surprised to hear Darling repeat the word hello on the other end of the line.

"You good?" Shantay asked Jill one last time before she fixed a plate and took off. "Thanks for the snack!" She winked at Jill and Jill winked back.

DOWN ON THE FARM

Jill suddenly felt the insatiable urge to call up an old friend to tell her all about the good news she just got from Darling and so she dialed up Twila, a woman at least ten years her senior, who sang in the church choir with her dad way out in the sticks, back in Ohio.

"Hello, Hello?" Twila answered the call on the first ring as if she could not hear the voice on the other end of the line.

"Hello? Oh my God! Twila can you hear me? How are you?" Jill asked.

"Oh, I can't complain." Twila said before she began complaining.

"Well, listen to this shit!" Jill was ready to dive headlong into their conversation before Twila quickly interrupted with questions.

"Are you down on the farm?" She sounded whipped out and winded. "Had to walk clear across the fields to get back to the house. Good thing I grabbed the flip phone out of the Subaru. We got stuck in the mud over there by Harper's farm so we had to hoof it home."

"So guess what? I moved back to Chicago, Twila! Can you believe it? I really did and again, after all these years, and it feels fantastic! You know weed is legal here. You can buy it all over the place!"

"Oh, well," Twila brushed off that comment sounding beyond disappointed that Jill had not come to visit her on the farm. "Well, you just sound so close by is all." She grumbled. "I thought you might be over at your dad's or something."

"Well, I guess that's just the miracle of modern technology!" Jill laughed out loud. "I do wish I was there right now though so that we could hang out at the fair again like we did last summer.

The county fair is the best thing going out in cow country, always has been, hands down! Well, that, and the fireworks on the Fourth of July!

Oh, how I do miss the smell of deep fried county fair food wafting through the summer sky, elephant ears as big as your head, fried ice cream, foot long corn dogs, pastel paper cone sticks wrapped in cotton candy for days, the sheen of the metallic paint from the bumper cars glistening in the sun after it rains as the sky casts a rainbow over all those bright neon lights surrounded by a shroud of total darkness with no street lights for hours. Getting tossed around on the Scrambler before it happens all over again between the sheets that night. Sex really is the perfect summertime activity. Muggy hot days, men in tight ripped jeans and tank tops sporting a million tattoos all up and down their sun-baked guns on full tilt strutting around in those snakeskin shit kickers chewing on blades of grass. You know, the memory of that alone made life down there worth living and personally I would love to go for a roll in the hay with one of them hillbillies again! I really would!"

"Oh my! Well, apple pie and God bless America!" Twila belted out the funny phrase as only a good all American gal knew how to do. "When you put it that way it really does make this town sound exciting but, you know, I never did get to ride the Scrambler much if you get where I am coming from with that."

"I see, said the blind man." Jill responded, making Twila laugh like crazy. "Twila, you do know that I write fiction for a living right?"

"Oh right! Your family is just so creative and talented." Twila said. "Especially your dad."

"Well, I could probably write travel brochures about the country if I really wanted to, but basically I just pulled those memory straight out of my ass just now and then spit them straight out of my hot chili hole but that's all just between you, me and the porcelain bowl I just made Hershey's kisses in." Jill joked around with her fun friend as she searched high and low for her one-hitter.

"Well you know how I love me some chili," Twila played along before she started talking about something totally unrelated, like she always did, reminding herself over and over again, out loud, about all the shit she thought she needed to do that day, shit that nobody else gave a hoot about except for her, because that was just her way of reminding herself that she had reasons to get out of bed every morning since she was on disability.

"I got to get my crock pot back from Linda. She took it last month to make them peanut butter rice crispy treats for the grandkids. I haven't seen her since and I'll tell you that really burns my ass when people borrow stuff and don't bring it back. The nerve of that cow." Twila complained.

In the meantime Jill's eyeballs were scanning the empty refrigerator standing in front of her face. "This fridge is always empty, FUCK!" She vented. "I am constantly running out of food here even though it feels like I spend every waking moment hauling ass over to the Jewel with a damn cart to grab groceries because I don't have a car anymore."

"Oh Mylanta!"

"Look, I had to give it up when I moved back to the city because apparently it was a total waste of space, just like me, and so basically I've been hoofing it everywhere I go too and it's getting old real fast. I must have been bonkers and out of my gourd to think that I was going to move back here and survive this city, as an older version of my fabulous self, and without a car, yet sadly here we are! I mean WHAT was I thinking Twila? I am totally exhausted all the time, I mean literally! What in the fuck?"

"Yeah, well," Twila returned to obsessing over her own life, "We got to figure out how to get that sucker out of the ditch because I got to drive back over to the food bank later this week cause first they tried to give me a bunch of expired food, which I returned, and then they ran out of them kipper snacks they usually have so they said to stop back in Friday to see if they get another donation in by then so I'll be do that, I guess. Also they left the celery out of the bag and baking in the sun so now that is limp as a wet noodle and I just can't believe they gave me expired meat again, those bastards!"

"Wait...couldn't you just call over there and ask Stacey to drop the kippered snacks off at your front door and bring you fresh celery since you live right down the road from her?"

"Not anymore! Didn't you hear? Stacey and Ed are getting a divorce and he put a restraining order on her and everything on a count of he got to the courthouse first to file and she couldn't find
an advocate to help her do one too because the court house was closed by the time she made it down there so She can't go near that house anymore."

"WHAT in the actual fuck?" Jill slammed the fridge door shut hard enough to shake the shit off a shingle.

Twila continued to gossip. "She's been staying over there in Rusty's double-wide off Dotlon, behind the Dollar General. Virginia said there hasn't been any funny business going on and she lives over there with her twin sister too, so she would know."

"Is that right? Now wait a minute, hold your horses, didn't Ed just knock Stacey up last year too? Christ!"

"And the year before that, and the year before that." Twila added. "Hell, if I had a lotto ticket for every time he plowed down on that poor girl I'd be richer than Sadie James."

"Sadie James?" Jill asked.

"Oh she was the one that won the power-ball grab last month over in Indiana." She said in the local paper that was gonna be her retirement plan since her family home burned down in that fire with her whole family in it. I think she deserved a little good luck after all that terrible shit happened to her, don't you?"

"Well, I'm still shocked as shit about what a pig that fat old fuck Ed turned out to be!"

"Oh, my lord, yes! And she was barely legal when he started porking her but I guess that is besides the point. She used to take all the calls over there at the food bank but since Ed cut her phone service off last week.

I need to stop over there to get the scoop in person about all that cheating business that has been going on. I know, for a fact, that she is gonna be there and then I am going to ask her, point blank, what really happened between her and Ed because well, inquiring minds want to know, and besides, I know she is gonna spill the beans because she already told uncle Donnie about all this and he told me she had a real bad case of the baby blues after Jameson was born so Ed wound up gettin' real horny so he turned around and started cheating on her with Lisa, that land snatch who works nights out there at the Pure gas station off 101, and boy is *she* a piece of shit!

I heard she was dancing for dollars down there at the *Lucky Strike* but I doubt it because she couldn't even afford to pay her heating bill last winter, on account of all them painkillers she was popping. She almost died you know. She took her four kids and a few of them chickens they raised and moved over there to Willy's old place in town, and she didn't want the pipes to freeze up so she was using the stove to heat the place. But then uncle Donnie said she blew the whole front porch off that rental and all their chickens went flying everywhere when that gas stove caught fire but I heard they ate them chickens before they could fly the coop.

That family never did seem to have enough food to go around because she was too lazy to get off her stupid ass and go to the food bank, like the rest of us and her car kept breaking down. So anyways, I guess Ed offered to stop over there after work one day and board the porch up for her because it was the middle of winter and them kids were freezing their asses off over there, so I guess he put on his tool belt and went to work, and took care of business, so to speak, so now she is pregnant again."

"Is she? Oh my word! How big *is* Ed's tool belt anyways Twila? Because I heard all kinds of wild stuff about his wiener over at the VFW hall after Chrystal and I, we got done swimming at the pool on that day the bugs got really bad the last time I was down on the farm."

"Jill! Now you know good girls never tell tales out of school. And besides, I don't remember how big his wiener was but I have seen some real monsters in my day and you know what they say about how they grow them boys big down here in cow country!"

"Amen to that! You ain't lying!" Jill exclaimed as Twila giggled like a giddy school girl.

"You hear Darrel nearly got his yang stripped off when he pulled his pappy's big tractor out of the barn?"

"Oh no!" Jill laughed uncontrollably "What the hell are you talking about now?"

"Well, I heard he has got a pair of them droopy dog sized balls you know, the ones that hang real low and sway back and forth and wobble to and fro and smack up against your inner thighs like a red turkey waddle when they walk?"

"You don't say…say more!"

"Well, I kept telling that boy to pull his pants up past his ass cracks but he thinks he's hot shit. Well, I guess he got sloppy with his junk one day and hopped up there on the tractor in them low riders and got his nut sack all jammed up in the machinery like a balloon animal that some kids was about to explode with his greasy little fingers twisted around it, so then his pappy had to cut him loose from that mess and they tossed him in the mail truck that was over yonder sitting at the gate and drove him down past the runoff pond and into town to see Doc Willy."

"And?"

"That's the whole story. So, anywho, I have to tell you I was thinking about you the other day at the county fair. There I was, standing at the main gate waiting on Dale to park the truck out past the stadium because, you know, they had to set up the Scrambler on the other side of the fun house this year cause of all that rain they got and the 4H had to change which barn they voted for the heifers in too, because I guess there was a whole shit ton of dung around the big barn and there were people out there stop, drop, and rolling, tripping and falling all over each other like pigs in a puddle in that mess until Grady pulled up and dumped hay bails off the back of his truck bed to soak up all that shit."

"So what are you trying to say Twila? You kind of lost me there. Are you trying to say that I remind you of cow dung because…"

"Oh heavens no!" Twila howled while snorting Crystal Light up her nostrils. "Let me grab a toot and my dip can so I can take a pinch and I'll be right back, okay sis? I'm feeling rather shitty and full so I may have to take a dump too, just hold your horses."

Great! Lovely visual Twila, truly, thanks for that.

Jill drank the rest of the warm, flat Pepsi out of the two-liter she found on the floor after her friend left to relieve herself.

"So anyways. I'm back! Sorry! I had to hop in the tub real quick and rinse off my backside because Dale forgot to buy toilet paper again. But anyways, I was over there waiting on him, at the fair, when I passed up the ball toss with the mini fish bowls with the fancy fighter fish swimming in food coloring, and they were giving away them rainbow colored hair clips, that you like, as prizes and that made me think of you."

"Twila, you are aware that those are not REALLY hair clips right? They are roach clips which are used to smoke weed and all those colors actually represent the gayness that we out here in liberal land like to call pride."

"Well, they can call it whatever they want out there in Chiraq but you are never going to catch me dead wearing one of them silly things in my hair because God teaches us that drugs and homosexuality are the devil's doing."

"Okay, Twila. You know, I really *do* have some great news that I want to tell you now!" Jill quickly changed the subject in an effort to talk about anything other than the devil.

"I just got back from the food bank and I can't carry all them groceries inside with my back the way it is now so I left Dale's beer and them day old hot dogs in the back of the Subaru but I don't want them baking in the sun all day neither. Dale must have rode over to the neighbors. Either that or he drove the riding mower into town to top off the tank because I don't hear him out there anymore which reminds me that I need to stick that can of beer I popped in my purse in the fridge so there is a cold one ready for him when he gets done digging those post holes. Now that is a big job! He's such a good boy! Do you think your dad wants any of them hot dogs I got for the root beer stand he helped set up in front of the grocery store? I saw the sign they had up that said 'now accepting donations' but I didn't notice the sign out there today unless they are using it for something else now. Have you heard from your dad lately? Has he called you?"

"No Twila, he hasn't. I don't really even know what phone number he is using these days, he has had so many different burner phones. He dropped one of them in a volcano."

"Well, I haven't seen his truck over there at the house lately either but I did see Betty's blue bug parked over at his duplex about a month back when his truck was there too. I wonder if she was over there getting paid to clean the place for him. I just can't imagine her getting down on her hands and knees like that but maybe he was having new tenants move in so he required her services."

"Who?"

"Betty, you know, Harold's wife. She is married, you know. That lady they got to sing over there at the tent revival they set up in that empty lot across from the Ponderosa and everyone said she sang like a songbird, but I didn't think so at all. I thought her voice was more of a piercing trill and the whole time she was singing I just wanted her to shut that pretty little pie hole of hers. Now, I never sang as a professional or in any sort of paid choir but I guess they said they needed her high-pitched voice to counterbalance the tone of your father's deep bass. I mean, I bet he really can go low."

"ANYWAYS Twila, I really wouldn't contact him about donating those wieners. I mean, who knows where the hell he is anyways. I wish I was there because I would gladly help you carry the rest of the groceries inside. I miss hanging out with you so much!"

"Well bless your heart, Jill! You are just such a treasure! Are you driving down for Thanksgiving? We are having a potluck dinner over at Christ church this year. I guess your dad's been over there a couple times before at the ice cream social because Gladys told me his favorite flavor is butter pecan and I guess he really fancies Cindy May's world-famous tacos. He never touches my taco."

"Excuse me? Did you hear what you just said to me?" Jill nearly peed herself laughing.

"Well, anyways, tell him to stop over when he is in town again. There is no sign for that church off the main road, but he knows how to get there. You know where Bobby's farm is on the corner by the county home where we did that community service together once to get food stamps?"

"Yes" Jill rolled her eyes.

"Well anyways, it is across the road there, down past the greenhouse, past the pole barn. But if you pass the railroad tracks then you have gone too far. It's the church where they had that walking tour of the reenactment of the resurrection of Christ last Easter. Come to think of it, I think it was your dad who played God in that revival and boy did he steal THE show!"

"My dad playing God? Huge shock. Jill secretly smiled.

"Oh, but you should have seen him! He looked so angelic up there dangling from the rafters in that contraption he fashioned out of chicken wire and feathers he found out by the burn pile in the back yard. He is just so creative and clever..."

"Oh wow, Holy Shit!"

"What happened?" Twila asked

"Well you know that good news I was getting ready to tell you about?"

"I think so..."

"Well, I just got it! This up and coming Chicago comedian

just texted me. She hired me to write stand-up comedy for her, for a major VIP charity event that she is hosting here in the city. A twenty-five hundred dollar advance just hit my online bank account!!!"

"Who is this character? A female carrot top?"

"No silly goose!" Jill roared with laughter

"Amy Schumer?"

"Not that east coast clown!"

"Oh my!"

"A CHICAGO comedian, Twila. Pay attention now! One more strike and you are officially out!" Jill pretend threaten her friend.

"Okay, Tina Fey!"

"No. She moved to the dark side years ago. It's Darling Radcliff."

"Who the hell is that?" Twila sounded confused.

"The comedian who just transferred money into my account, that's who! Hell YES!!!! Twila, can I call you back later? I can feel some heavy retail therapy coming on and it's about to last all day long." Jill gasped as she rubbed her red eyes to do a double take at her new bank balance.

"Oh Jill, you know you can call me anytime day or night sweetheart!"

"Thanks, Twila. I have no friends in the city yet so that really means a lot to me. It is such a magnificent day outside for shopping!"

"Well then, get out there and play in the sunshine already. That is God's gift because the sun shines on all of us equally you know?"

"Amen to Sunshine! Well, I am off to shop on the Magnificent Mile, I am going to waltz right into Nordstrom, and splurge on this fabulous pair of sunglasses wrapped in black leather that I have had my eyes on ever since I landed on the Gold Coast. You know, I have been channeling Chanel all summer long. I swear I must have walked over to Nordstroms a half a dozen times to look at the same pair and now they are mine, all mine! Holy shit! I never thought this would happen to me! I am so beyond psyched."

WHAT IS SO FUNNY ABOUT MENOPAUSE?

Jill felt like she had died and gone straight to heaven on the first day of fall as she entered a lavish courtyard overflowing with flowers of every kind and Ginkgo trees whose leaves had just turned the richest shade of gold—her favorite color.

She had been invited by Darling to an event she was headlining for Menopause Day that was taking place that afternoon.

There Jill was, standing in the sunshine, shoulder to shoulder with some of the most important and influential women in the windy city all dressed in dazzling attire, laughing uproariously at the jokes that she had written for the hottest comedy act in town.

Jill was having a blast letting the sound of laughter follow her around like the singing birds in Cinderella, as she floated through the crisp autumn air in a glitzy rent-the-runway gown, paired with those chic Chanel shades, laced in leather, that she had been fantasizing about possessing for so long until she finally broke down and bought them. The first meaningful keepsake of value that she had purchased on her own dime.

She was listening to the tail end of the comedy act as she approached the bar to order a libation. She was paying close attention to the way Darling delivered every line in the way that Jill had rehearsed it when she penned the act.

She fondly recalled the way that Darling had insisted that she make up catchy titles for each comedy bit. *Well, now that she has bits to go with all of her bobbles, she must be pleased as punch!* Jill congratulated herself for a job well done as she watched the comedian clutch the sides of the microphone with her delicate finger tips as she inched closer and closer to it as if she was about to reveal some dirty little secret she wanted everyone to know. She paused briefly, for effect, before continuing her performance.

"Ladies, I want to talk about THE CHANGE and what it feels like to fuck over 50, because I was that dumb drunk that forgot to bring her own lube to the party because nobody ever tells you this shit when you hit menopause like the fact that there will be no more chasing waterfalls for my ladies from the 80's, not for long, so make sure you cum prepared, if you know what I mean. She began tossing free bottles of lube to the ladies standing in the growing crowd.

And yes, you can be dry as a dessert and pissed off as a python about to strike at anyone who comes closer than the CDC's recommended six feet of your menopausal ass. I am just grateful they put that rule in place before THE CHANGE hit me and I turned into a total monster.

The CHANGE is that confusing time in life when you tend to adopt that love them and leave them mentality for the first time in your life because the bottom line is that you want that wiener but what you don't want is that hot blooded hairy Sasquatch that ding dong is attached to.

Okay, so let's just say, for shits and giggles, that you just got some dick and then you drank all his tequila and you thought you were feeling pretty good until the hot flashes that you are about to receive really kick into high gear sending you into bitch mode maximum overdrive. You know, part of that condition the doctor warned you about before he suggested that you look into taking behavioral therapy.

"Okkkkkkurrrrr?????????" Darling used a phrase from the show
which Jill wrote for Soda Pop Pink, which she then accidentally performed live, which quickly went viral on social media.

Darling was psyched to be reaching a wider audience that included women from other generations thanks to that funny mix-up that happened which inadvertently lead to an increase in her popularity as a live performer.

"Where my gen Z fans at? Holla! How you vibing tonight?" Darling scanned the audience for answers. "Okay, I just heard someone boo hiss me, who was that? Speak now or forever fuck off." She shouted with glee as she threw up her middle finger and the crowd broke out in laughter.

"Slaying!" Somebody screamed and then Darling reacted by revealing her famous British buck teeth as she smiled ear to ear.

"Well, if you are harassing me because I wasn't acting my age the last time you saw me that really wasn't my fucking fault.

In the meantime, Jill was standing at the bar, peaking over the top of her shades, listening to Darling bring her stories to life as she tried, in vain, to grab the attention of someone, any of the staff members standing behind the bar, because she was ready to order a drink.

Suddenly, a handsome Mediterranean man appeared from out of nowhere.

"I am here to serve you," He said.

Jill was gobsmacked for moments, by what he said, but when she finally came to her senses she spontaneously responded. "Well! That is fantastic, but first, somebody needs to cut that audience off, quick! I think they've had too much to drink, don't you think? I mean, come on! Those jokes can't be all THAT funny...or can they? Gi, Gi, Giovanni?" Jill struggled to read the gentleman's name tag as she squinted into the fading sun.

"Ferrari, Giovanni Ferrari." The handsome stranger, who was wearing an Armani suit, introduced himself to Jill last name first, as if he were Bond, James Bond.

Jill slowly removed the gold-fringed mask she was wearing to reveal the right shade of rouge that she had selected to stain the apples of her high cheekbones with before this major event.

She then slowly reached across the bar to pluck a single glazed cherry out of a blown glass bowl sitting next to a twisted stack of napkins, tastefully arranged on the rock solid granite counter-top.

She sucked the red ball off that dangling piece of low fruit like a Dyson, right in front of Gio. She was carefully extracting all of its sweet juices before she jerked the stem off to transform it into the perfect lovers knot with one slippery twist of her tantalizing tongue.

"Wow, a wee wa!" Gio exclaimed as Jill slowly pulled the long stem from her mouth to twirl it between her slippery fingers.

"Got to lube it up! That's what she said."

"Wow! That is some cool party trick! Did you go to school to learn how to do that?" Giovanni Ferrari was clearly flirting too.

"No, I went to school to study Italian eyes." Jill gazed deep into his.

"Good guess!" He said. "My parents were born in Sicily." He sliced a fruit to add to her sweet libation.

"So, what was your major in school?" She asked.

"Theater, and believe you me, I know a good performance when I see one, and THAT is true talent!" He pointed to Darling who was still standing on the stage.

"Is that a fact?" Jill smirked. "Because actually…" She was about to reveal her superpower when Gio interrupted her to say something else she found flattering.

"Look, there is simply nothing sexier than a woman who speaks her mind. It's as simple as that!" He said. "Plus, she gets paid for her opinions? Major bonus and major boner" He added, "Smart lady, and very funny, unlike most women I know who say they are hilarious but they are not."

"Oh, really? Would you go so far as to say that she is hysterical?" Jill pressed.

"Yes! As a matter of fact, I would go that far." He said.

"How far do you want to go?" She practically jumped over the bar to attack him with kisses. "Say more!" were the next words out of her perfect pout as she encouraged Gio to continue engaging her in this witty banter while she slowly slipped her hand down the front of her gown, reaching first base with herself, as she yanked a one dollar bill out of her bra to shove it into the slit on the top of the tip jar but alas the vessel already blew its wad evidenced by the tips that were spilling out all over that rock-solid wet bar that had been erected for this funny affair. Jill knew the only thing that stood between her and Gio now was something very hard indeed.

"Sorry, this one is a little limp." After removing the bill from her bra Jill rubbed it across the stiff surface of the counter before attempting to cram it in the tight slit, on the top of the tip jar, but to no avail.

"Well, I guess we'll just let this one air out" She said before the dollar bill blew away. "Well, no matter. After all, I see your cup already overfloweth my liege!" Jill dropped her discarded cherry stem next to the twenty dollar bills scattered over the rest of the bar.

She was starting to wonder if she was ever going to get laid again or if she was actually going to have to pay for it this time around and that is when Darling approached the bar to join her friend for a drink.

"Well, hello funny lady with the fancy frock." Darling playfully bumped hips with Jill who instantly obliged by bumping hips back.

Gio interrupted this merrymaking to ask Jill if she was going to introduce him to her friend, while he popped the top on the She Can that Darling ordered, sliding it across the bar to her as he made full eye contact.

"Look, you had your chance to meet the talent and you blew it."
So, get bent fuck boy! AM SCRAM!" Jill blew her stack at Gio using pig Latin while lashing out which typically indicated that she was, in fact, having a hot flash due to drinking.

"Don't you love it when a woman speaks her mind?" Darling asked Gio as she raised her She Can high in the air to toast her sidekick Jill as if they were playing off each other's antics in a team comedy sketch. Darling took two satisfying sips of that lip-smacking wine before she spoke. "I find this scenario simply refreshing. I really do!"After she pounded the wine, she crushed the She Can on her forehead before pushing it back across the bar to request another drink from Gio without making eye contact.

"Oh, that reminds me." Jill said. "You really were crushing it out there!" She complimented Darling. "No pun intended."

"Speaking of true talent AND introductions…" Darling said to Jill. "It would be both an honor and a privilege to introduce you to some of my influential art friends who work in the business." She quipped. "You know, people with real jobs." She said as she locked eyes with Gio who tried to busy himself by doing other things. "I mean, if you are up for that type of tomfoolery." She offered Jill the crook of her arm as they skipped away together.

***

"Ahoy mateys, now hear this my fellow merry makers." Darling drew a lot of attention as she attracted an audience of other artists who began to form a circle around her.

"Let me tell you a story!" Darling always started off strong because she knew how to grab the attention of her audience. "But first!" She said before saying something to an artist that she knew who was standing across from her and was somebody who she happened to know. "Cyan, I hear you are raising a few zoomers from generation NEXT and they just turned teenager."

Cyan was sporting a pair of mustard yellow high top Chuck Taylor sneakers with pumpkin spice orange leg warmers. She had accessorized with chunky jewels in fall tones and painted cat eyes like Priscilla Presley on her face. She was donning a free flowing caftan with vivid and wild comic book characters printed randomly all over the free flowing piece that hung from the bold frame of her body in an inspirational asymmetrical fashion.

"Generation what exactly are you talking about? You know you make these kids sound like they came from outer space or some shit," Cyan said. "And, Lord Jesus help us, I am raising these twins all alone ever since their dad decided I was too old for him."

"Seriously?" Jill responded.

"As serious as I can be for a comedian!" Cyan said. "you know, laughter is all I have left."

"You know what Cyan," another comic from the group named Lyric chimed in. "For a woman who does not actually go to church anymore, you sure do pray to Jesus a lot."

"Well, you know Lyric, for someone who does go to church," Cyan barked back. "You sure are the nosiest bitch in the bunch and super judgy!"

"Let it go ladies!" Darling insisted. "I just need an answer to one question. What is up with this hair they wear in every color of the rainbow, these Zoomers? I mean, is that suppose to be sexy or cute because I don't want to fuck a Muppet, Do you?"

All the ladies broke out in laughter as if it had been more contagious than Covid.

"It's like a generation reduced to nothing more than a barf bag full of Skittles, I tell ya." Darling felt like she was on a roll as she took another sip of her fine wine.

"She does have a point!" Cyan snickered. "And don't you know, these Zoomers ARE trying to start shit with me every day all the time, like that day they told me they had no use for pronouns anymore since they were going to start identifying as unicorns.

The only problem with that is that these fools are identical twins. Makes no fucking sense to me point blank. You know what? Come to think off it, maybe these kids were sent from outer space to fuck with us!" Cyan pulled a vape pen out of her housecoat to hit it hard.

"Let me tell you a story." Darling addressed the group again.

"I brought up the subject of these Zoomers only because I recently experienced my own encounter with a social media influencer from generation Z and that was totally bizarre.

This story all started after I decided I wanted to perform my menopause comedy on stage but I was going through THE CHANGE myself so I needed someone to help me write it, to help punch up some of the jokes before I performed it, because I had a bad case of brain fog at the time and it could have been from multiple things.

"Wow, what a novel idea. A comedian telling a story I can actually relate to. I do appreciate you!" Cyan said to Darling as she raised her glass to the She Can.

"I am certain you ladies must be aware that I love to make a huge splash when it comes to all things comedy and really rock the boat, right?" Darling continued.

"Right!" All onlookers agreed.

"Make a statement that matters! Go big or go home! I just want to dive off the deep end headfirst, to boldly go where no comedian has ever gone before. I am not interested in sticking my toes in the water to see if it is wet. I am going to stick my whole foot in that fucking drink.

The pandemic all but turned this city into a joker-less concrete jungle and I, for one, fully intend to take advantage of the comedy renaissance we are currently experiencing.

Clearly I had every intention of writing my own comedy but the hits just kept coming, in the form of a hormone imbalance, with emotions and feelings that I could not control, and I can't take hormones due to the history of breast cancer in my family.

So anyway, one day when I could not bear living through the

hell of feeling hot and cold and hot and cold all of the time I just knew that I needed to reach out and ask for help.

At first I thought it was Covid that gave me the brain fog and so I was just putting myself out there, walking around town in a complete daze, thinking, 'this too shall pass,' but still refusing to go to the doctor to find out what was really wrong with me because nobody went to the doctor last year unless they got deathly ill. And since people were dropping dead like flies everywhere, I just felt super silly dialing up my PC to complain about female trouble. But I really did feel like I was losing my noodle all the time until I had to make an executive decision to just live with myself, flaws and all, and just take a step back from the spotlight and relax instead of trying to control my erratic moods all the time. And *that* is when I knew that I needed to take a break from all the stress of being a real woman by just letting these warm waves of calm energy wash over my weary body, and that is when I started investing in some serious self-care."

"Now, why didn't I think of that?" Cyan gave herself a prat slap on the forehead for effect.

"So, I designated a few nights of the week for self care and I started to take that shit super seriously and really pamper myself. I started to treat myself like the queen I always knew I was. I gave myself pedicures, painted my toenails Bahamas Blue, and indulged in ordering my favorite coconut cake drizzled in Curacao from the London House. In fact, once a week, I would have it delivered to my door and then I would devour it immediately and take a long ass nap. But, it was only after *all* of that—as I was laying there all sprawled out on my bed, slick as a seal, freshly showered and shaved, with my ceiling fan set on high, listening to that song 'Sailing,' by Christopher

Cross, letting the song take me away to a place where I wished I was going when it dawned upon me that I should send out an SOS immediately to seek support, for my writers block, from someone in my tribe and that is when I dialed up my mentor Mary Gold.

"I reached out to hire her to write for me but she graciously declined my offer. She said she was flattered that I was thinking of her for the project but she had someone else in mind and no time to take on extra clients because her fourth divorce had just been finalized and she was packing her bags to be whisked away on this romantic cruise she was taking with her new lover, Roman, who she met on IG. He lives on an island.

"Anyway, instead of blowing me off completely, she did me a favor first. She introduced me to her other protege who I had no idea even existed, until now, by the way, and her name is Jill." She then introduced her ghostwriter friend to her fellow artists. "She writes brilliant comedy!"

"Did I hear someone say comedy writer for hire?" A long-legged lady stuck her neck in the circle to join in on the conversation. Jill had to do a double take before it sunk in that this sailor clown was wearing an all-white suit, post Labor Day, with a pair of matching patent leather loafers on her huge feet that had gold-plated anchors attached to the front of them.

"Got a card, skipper?" The crane neck in the captain's cap asked Jill. "My name is Ah Bologna, by the way." She introduced herself by raising her hand to initiate a fist pump with Jill.

"You're kidding right? I mean, about your name?" Jill said.

"Nope. That's my name. Don't wear it out!" Ah Bologna

taunted Jill as if they were in grade school.

"Sorry, but no." Jill said. "I am not officially a card-carrying member off clown club."

"Yet!" The skipper said. "You should always add that word to the end of every sentence you utter. I find it makes life more interesting, really."

Jill gave the comedian a fist bump back saying "right on! Not yet then." She reminded herself that she needed to wash her hands, like a million times, as soon as she had the chance to slip away from all that silliness.

As Ah Bologna drew back her fist she let it explode into five fingers like a cherry bomb. "Wow! You do know that you are blowing my mind sailor," she said, "I mean literally! What kind of a shit bird comes to a networking gig without a calling card? I mean what *is* this? Amateur hour?" She was really yucking it up.

"Nice pants. I hope you don't get your period." Jill clapped back based on a joke she heard before and soon she felt like she was on a roll. "What the hell is this nautical theme you two clowns cooked up, like your castaways dressed for a 51/50 intake on *Gilligan's Island* or something?" Jill openly roasted Darling and Ah Bologna in front of all their friends, which they got a total kick out of as opposed to finding the entire it insulting.

"Oh, this one has a silver tongue I see, very nice." Ah Bologna pointed out something about Jill as they continued to spar. "You want to battle? Which side of the city do you live on?" Ah Bologna was challenging Jill to a battle of the best neighborhoods as she pranced around her, taking playful jabs at her from every angle, like Popeye at a prizefight. "So, you like to riff and roast, do you?" She taunted her new rival.

"Stand down, sailor! Darling interjected. "Jill is in the right here Ah Bologna. We *were* on the sailing *and* the diving team together in Washington. We were both born water signs, in the Salish Sea on opposite islands. We have sailing in our blood and the sea in our veins and the mermaid fins to prove that we are islanders!" Darling proudly pontificated about their childhood.

"It's Ah Bologna, you know spelled like the sandwich-making meat," the comedian leaned in to tell Jill. "If you really must know what's with the name, *mine* is an homage to that zany expression about pretentious nonsense." She added "You know, when someone says something and you know they are full of shit so you just say "Ah Bologna! And I can smell it a mile away." She said as she sniffed Jill's shoulders.

Darling picked up her story where she left off, before she was interrupted, by saying. "Anyways, back to my story. Now pay close attention here, because class is in session, and I am already a little tipsy but if I keep having to repeat myself, and start telling this shit over and over again, this is going to sound like *The Never Ending Story* that never ends so please, listen up!"

"I mix things up, remember? That is where you left off," Jill kindly reminded Darling about the story she was telling.

"Oh yes!" Darling declared, flipping the Monet-inspired Water Lilies scarf she was wearing over her right shoulder, in a sweeping gesture as if she was about to reclaim her rightful thrown on the soap box because such was the life of a stand-up comedian who was always on.

"My point is, that you are not alone," Darling stated

emphatically. "We are *both* going through 'the change,' struggling to cope with the hormone-free hell some of us put ourselves through in an attempt to remain cancer-free. That complete inability to focus on a task at hand, any task, no matter how small, all from going through menopause is all consuming. You simply feel incapable, incapacitated even.

It is a dark cloud that makes you stress over every little every little task that needs doing in a day which is why, I believe, Jill accidentally mixed up that comedy she wrote for me with the material that was meant to be performed by a completely different kind of entertainer all together."

"Oh really? And, what kind of entertainer is that, pray tell? Cyan asked, pulling an E-cigarette out of her deep pocket to smoke it as she contemplated the nature of her own question.

"The *other* performer is this new age type of social media megastar by the name of Soda Pop Pink. She is Gen TikTok." announced Darling.

"So wait, you were performing live comedy that was written for someone else?"

"I was!" Darling said.

"Oh my God, that is fucking hilarious. I have to watch that reel! Where did this happen? Like, which clubs on what night? Now you have to spill the tea!" Cyan insisted.

"The Calamity Club on Clark is where this all went down live." Darling added. "I cannot remember where Soda Pop was performing, earlier that evening, but it was on the same night and the craziest part of this all was that some random Zoomer was attending my show, likely with her mother, when this comedy mix-up occurred, so she recorded the entire thing on her iPhone and posted it on every social media platform and she has a shit ton of followers.

Then, videos of both performances went viral, because you can't watch one without seeing the other, and the rest is history and comedy gold! So then I caught the attention of Soda Pop Pink's PR team, who recently hired me to fly out to L.A. to star in the Soda Pop Pink podcast starring Soda herself."

"Oh wow, how exciting. Congratulations!" Darling said. "What is the name of this podcast? I must keep an eye out for it."

"Well, the episode is actually called 'Damn Boomers are dumb!' Darling revealed the crazy title. "So, I have that going for me and who cares if she got my generation confused with the Boomers. I mean, hell, all the Zoomers think if you are over 35 you are old anyways and you know how they say if you can't beat them, join them, right?" Darling continued "We all make mistakes and I just do not have the energy to go around correcting slackers all the time. Besides, all this comedy confusion could lead to that big break I need to further brand myself by enhancing my social media presence, gaining followers, and doing all that other silly shit that society deems necessary nowadays for a comedian to remain relevant. Wow, it is truly sad what this world has come to, it truly is."

"On that note," Jill excused herself from the circle to escape to the restroom, where she could go to get a life online.

The moment Jill stepped into the powder room she lost her balance and fell to the floor in a drunken stupor. The next thing she remembers she awoke to a group of giggling girls who asked her if she needed any help getting up to which she promptly replied that she needed to set up a TikTok and IG account ASAP. They helped her create the accounts rickety-split, before they vanished into the stall next door to light up a joint.

Jill checked the time on her watch. It was 4:20, so she pulled out her Sunday Brunch hybrid vape and took a few puffs off it in the spirit of celebrating that particular moment in time before she returned to the artist circle with her social media presence fully established and ready to compete with the best in the business.

BLOOD MONEY

For the third time in three days, Jill was busy buying weed for the next two weeks, when Ah Bologna shot her a message on IG asking her what she would charge to write comedy for one of her new shows.

Jill was standing in line at the Sunny dispensary at the time and she was too far gone amusing herself with the antics of others, by people watching, to bother responding to this request right away. When she did eventually get around to messaging the comedian back, she simply quoted her a fee for services which was exactly the price that it would cost for her to buy back that gown she had worn to the menopause awareness event that she attended. She wanted it back for nostalgic reasons.

As luck would have it, she spotted that exact gown in a pop-up shop, on the Magnificent Mile while she was out taking a stroll one day. It had been marked down, at a deep, deep, discount, since it was now officially considered second-hand goods.

Jill was window shopping for shoes, to go with that gown she had just reclaimed when another comedian, from that same event where she was networking, messaged to ask her how much she would charge to write comedy for her new show as well.

However, then this most recent client made the mistake of giving Jill too much information which Jill took as a red flag because she did not really want to write for this woman anyways. The woman told Jill, point blank, that she preferred performing stand-up comedy over writing it any day of the week because she thought the writing part was so boring and there was nothing glamorous about it because it meant you were just holed up somewhere, hunched over a keyboard, in some crusty bathrobe, with only your own jokes to keep you company, dressed like some hobo in hiding, while the other comedians were out there performing and yucking it up with other comedians in real life, commingling with couples and singles alike, gallivanting around town, dressed in the latest fashion, sipping on signature cocktails, at the latest comedy clubs on the scene.

Jill responded to this comedian's inconsiderate rant by charging her, for comedy, the cost of a new pair of blood shoes that matched perfectly with the gown she had just reclaimed, making no bones about the price she quoted whatsoever, because she knew that every time she looked at the bottom of those bitches, from that point forward, she would be reminded of all the blood, sweat and tears she cried and the nights she had sacrificed, home alone, to climb that ladder of success that she was finally rising to the top of.

Nothing glamorous about this shit? I'll show you glamorous! Jill stepped into Christian Louboutin on Oak Street, like a boss bitch, to purchase yet another keepsake of craftsmanship and style to add to her growing collection of all things beautiful and beyond – or, as Jennifer Saunders would have put it with a cigarette dangling out of her mouth, "Her new collection of all things absolutely fabulous!"

Shantay admired the latest damage Jill did shopping when

she returned to the castle of her king on Lake Shore Drive. "Okay, so you think you are some kind of smooth operator now? You lasso yourself another high-dollar daddy with that tight pussy of yours Wonder Woman? DAMN! I mean, is that bean made of gold or something, sunshine?"

"Ca Va Shantay, so wonderful to see your radiant, glowing face today!" Jill greeted Shantay with the French expression she had just learned, at the designers boutique, as she stepped up to the stoop.

"Who needs a high-dollar daddy when you have got as much raw talent coursing through your veins, as I have?" Jill asked. "This girl is on fire! My career is on fire because I do the work that nobody else wants to do. Simple! The work that bores them to tears, I do. The work they refuse to do for fear that they might miss out on some social event they desperately want to attend. The work that leaves them so emotionally drained and utterly alone that they feel like they are going to lose their noodles. You know, Shantay, you should really read Franklin Covey." Jill continued.

"Speaking of losing your noodle, and your damn mind, I hope you got some groceries in those shopping bags you dragged in here, because the last time you passed out you were pale as a ghost, running around, talking gibberish, your cupboards were bare, and you were clearly not all together there." Shantay pointed out.

"Well, that may not have been my best day. But who has time to eat when you have a future as bright as mine to look forward to?" Jill threw her head back, laughing, in her fittingly named *Invincible* Chanel lipstick, as she ascended the lobby stairs.

"You really are a handful." Shantay said. "Let me buzz you in." She rolled her eyes up toward the five thousand dollar chandelier hanging over her head as she tapped on the button, behind the service desk to release the Kraken into the common area so she could collect her dry cleaning before she took the elevator all the way up.

Jill spent hours trying on her new designer digs as she danced through her lover's closet, in a purely euphoric state of mind, organizing everything by color as she admired how cheerful her closet felt which was clearly a reflection of her new lease on life.

She was chewing sugar-coated pineapple edibles while juggling a cup of bubble tea from TEAMO in one hand and pressing her cell phone against her cheek with her shoulder, to listen to voice messages, as she managed to balance articles of clothing on each of her outstretched arms as if she was a human coat hanger.

Later she found herself collapsed in that pile of clothes, on the closet floor, obsessing over a comment that some troll made on a reel of comedy she wrote.

HONEY CHILD

"So the online dating site HONEY claims to be a different kind of experience all together which is exactly how I would describe this sad and poorly designed platform.

They claim to be more female-friendly...and all that fake shit... until you find yourself matching with profiles in TRAVEL MODE and it took me a while to figure out what the hell that meant.

Okay, so according to HONEY 101, true story, because you DO actually need a virtual course to figure out
what the fuck all these trumped-up features they "offer" you actually mean in real life.

So Mandy or Karen or whoever, I can't keep track of their corporate team anymore because their turnover rate is so high, so whoever it is that works as the HONEY spokesperson posed this question, on their app, to singles who were ready to mingle.

"What if you are going on a business trip like a conference in Las Vegas, or something like that, only you want to start networking before you arrive?"

So, basically, these dating aficionados got together and decided it was a good idea to Geo-locate, and lump together, every last one of their TRAVEL MODE users together into one zip code, which happens to be mine, since I live near the airport and that is where these men are getting off, and I mean both literally and figuratively, and in every way possible. I mean some of these matches have even gone so far as to invite me on a date at an airport hotel where they are staying between flights.

So my canned response to all the Romeos stuck on travel mode reads like an office template I created at one of my many temporary contract jobs which reads like this:

I am not a tourist ATM. Do not come in my city and try to make a deposit and a withdrawal on your next layover."

COMEDIAN WALKS INTO A BAR

"A comedian walks into a bar on Halloween and the most handsome man that she has ever seen in her whole life is seated beside her.

He is just about to pay his tab and take off when he decides instead to strike up a conversation with her because he thinks she is kind of hot, which she is, in her own special way, because she is drinking. So, she tells him her name and he asks her what she does for a living.

"Who, me?" The woman seems shocked that he is giving her the time of day. "I write stand-up comedy for people with mental health problems and hot flashes."

"Jeez! What a job. How do you find the inspiration to write about all that stuff?" He asked.

"Good question!" she took the time to pay him a compliment before she overshared. "Most of it cums to me while I am masturbating in a shallow bath, the water pressure cranked up to an eleven, with my legs spread-eagle under the faucet.

I let the warm water rush over me in all the right places. After that I am inspired to write tons of shit so then I scribble ideas all over the tub walls, with my adult crayons. I have them in every color of the rainbow. I have the big box!

I generally emerge from this orgasmic experience all shriveled up like that old prune from *the Shining*, after I finish myself off, but it's generally well worth the fuss because that release transforms itself into comedy gold. And THAT is my superpower.

Why? Are you suddenly feeling the urge to come over to my place and get psycho with me sometimes?

Because that might be worth rehanging my shower curtain for."

THE DOORMEN

The other day I smashed the face on my brand-new smart phone to smithereens when my ankle snapped off sideways after I stepped down hard in a hole on the pavement right in front of the grocery store.

I was hangry as hell so I had been walking, fast as lightning in flip flops, because my stomach AND my fridge were empty and the cupboards were bare and nobody ever has a moment to spare, in the city, where you can never get enough good food to eat and there are rarely leftovers, like ever!

So, I am certain you can image how I was really in no mood to make small talk as I approached the doorman at the front desk, to buzz me into the building, on that particular day.

Nevertheless there he was, seated the same way he always was, on the daily, relaxing behind that plexiglass shield with his mask dangling down off his nose, kicking it in his usual spot

He was chatting it up on the business line with his lover, his ex-wife, his current wife, some trick, some rich, lonely and horny old resident, who the hell knows, with his legs fixed in a figure-four locked position crossed at the knee with one perfectly polished Oxford hanging high up into the air.

So, as I am walking through the lobby the OTHER doorman, the night doorman, steps up to the plate, in the booth, to relieve the windy city Casanova of his official duties doing next to nothing.

This night time doorman was a real piece of work too…

This poppy had sea-deep green eyes with a touch of brown speckles in them like the freckles that covered his smooth olive skin which stood in perfect contrast to the stiff upright standing cuff of his perfectly crisp collar and the shiny gold chains he was dripping with.

And to think that this exotic dream boat of a Latino man, who I later found out was in fact, from Cuba, once looked me dead in the eyes and told me he was white, and he was dead serious too.

So, I pulled up my sleeves, so we could compare arms next to one another. Mine was ghostly white compared to the rich copper tone of his radiant skin.

This did not matter to him because he had already convinced himself he was white which to this day blows my mind like nobody's business because the island gods clearly blessed this gentleman with the most unmistakable exotic beauty. One that you rarely find on the mainland.

This is how I learned, by the way, that everyone in the city wants to be somebody else. I mean I even do.

So, anyways, enough said about that and back to what happened next...

So Mr. Island exotic was busy schooling me on how I ought to be more careful and slow down next time I am out "walking the streets," is what he called it.

And he is saying all this because I just busted my ass and the glass on the face of my brand-new cell phone shattered so I was clearly devastated but I guess he just wanted to crack jokes, because that is the way Chicagoans release stress to lighten up any mood, by acting like a bunch of wise guys.

For some stupid reason I felt the need to further explain what happened and so I did so by saying...

"Look! I slipped into a hole. It was an accident."

On that note the Casanova, who is on the phone, hangs up with the caller, looks up at the other doorman and then they both look me dead in the eyes and in unison they say...

"That's what I told my wife!"

Jill thought this material that she was writing was all rather clever until she noticed that some troll had bothered to snide comment about her comedy in the comments.

"How is this funny?" the comment said. This was barely any sort of insult at all, but it was certainly insulting enough to make Jill feel like a total piece of shit as she dropped everything she was doing to let the devil back through the back door as she took a tailspin which sent her spiraling down the deepest and darkest of digital rabbit holes.

"My career is over, Dream," she said as she fell to pieces on the floor, forlorn at the sight of her own sad clown face in the vanity on the bathroom door.

She was crying her eyes out because she truly believed that there was no hope for the future of her own career. She remained like that, frozen in time, until sleep stole her away only to awaken to yet another miserable day.

She stirred before the sun and immediately grabbed her cell phone, without bothering to turn on the lights, and began to scroll, even though it was still pitch-black in the room.

She felt the urge to see if that comment that she saw was still there. It was. It existed but nobody else had commented on that comment. She also wanted to check back on the other comedy reels that her material appeared in to see if any of them got panned by some random asshole critic.

She forgot to blink as she scrolled, continuously checking for comments on reel after reel of comedy, to the point where it felt like she had fried the whites of her own eyeballs out, just like that 'This is your brain on drugs' commercial they played, back in the 80s. She could feel herself becoming addicted to this digital drug called social media as she progressively became more and more a former shell of herself, letting her online experiences control her IRL. Letting the glow of that bright screen suck her in like that poor kid in *Poltergeist.*

Jill felt a desperate desire to know what that troll meant by making that comment or if they just did that to start some unnecessary drama with her. Jill wanted to know if they had any fucking idea how hard it was to put yourself out there, the way she had, taking risks to express her true self to the world by writing comedy for a living. *Art was always such a gamble.*

She wanted to know, specifically, which joke and what part of that joke they were referring to exactly, or which part of what joke, or was it the punch line of one of them that they did not find funny?

Who was this shit starter who was trying to bait her anyways? And how was Jill to know if she had any respect for their sense of humor inn the first place? She did know one thing. They had posted enough useless, boring-garbage photos of backyard barbecues, on their profile page, to put anyone to sleep who was viewing their channel, so therefor they were just a nobody, like her.

She kept obsessing over one silly comment when she noticed that she was still wearing the clothes she had dressed up in the day before, only now they felt too snug against her skin. So she donned her sunglasses and took a very long walk.

EVEN IN CHANEL

Jill no longer had two fucks to give if it was light or dark outside as the yellow Ginkgo leaves began to fall from the trees outside, floated down to land on sidewalks where they collected along streets named after the great lakes, to muddy themselves in puddles filled with all the tears that Jill had cried, over the years, over too many worthless and forgettable men to count. She hid her face behind every pair of sunglasses she had ever worn as she walked the streets aimlessly, that windy city woman.

The thought then occurred to her, that it really did not matter who you were, or how rich, because the honest-to-God truth was that you could still be depressed, even in Chanel and there was no running from LOVE.

If she had seen that catch phrase printed on a billboard somewhere, it may have planted a seed inside her head, normalizing her mental illness long enough to let her learn to accept her diagnosis. But in real life, she knew she had never seen a sign like that in her life and that a city stopped for no one because it was its own source of eternal energy.

After walking that day, Jill stopped going outside altogether. She was beyond depressed. Her career was over and the weather was starting to turn, which meant that soon the flowers would all be dead in their metal casket beds, outside millions of skyscraper windows, as the light dimmed the sky like a switch.

SATAN, THE AIR BISCUIT

Jill felt bulbous, bloated, and full of hot air, wondering why the world was such a dark place, until it finally dawned on her that she was still wearing her sunglasses inside.

Just another brick in the wall, she thought as she leaned against the back of a blood red-sectional, martini glass in hand and tilted slightly sideways, as she stared up at the only patch of sun she had seen in a very long time.

It appeared in the shape of a golden waffle on the floor, as it filtered through the windows across the way, bouncing rays of joy into the condo like the cross-section of a glowing board game of X's and O's.

Jill was standing in that small patch of sun with her eyes closed, soaking up the rare rays as she blew smoke from her cigarette, allowing the yellow vapors to co-mingle with the dust particles that filled the stale air where she stood, all alone.

Without warning, the sun disappeared and Jill ripped the sunglasses off her face in a dramatic and sweeping manor that matched her mood. She threw them to the floor where they slid into a corner, collapsing in on themselves, cowering like that lion with no heart that she now believed her lover had become after all these years.

As cold as ice, he had effectively and efficiently iced her out lately, not communicating with her much at all, asking her just to text him instead of call, leaving her to wonder if she was simply out of sight and mind for him, unless they were banging one out for old times' sake as if he kept her in his drawers, like a pack of fresh batteries.

"May They Rest In Peace, along with this failed relationship." Jill performed the stations of the cross, kneeling over her sunglasses before she walked away to fall back on her lover's bed, where she fell fast asleep after playing a quick stare-me-down game with Dream, who had carefully selected a comfortable place to sleep on top of one of the many piles of dirty laundry that were growing out of the every corner of the room.

As the weather continued to take a turn for the worse, and the cold rain began to shit all over Chicagoland, Jill became increasingly agoraphobic, rarely leaving the condo for weeks on end. She continued to order groceries for delivery from Seven Eleven, cooking garbage processed food for herself every day and soon the calories began to pile up because she was no longer counting them or her many blessings. She continued to lay around in the bed and let her depression suck the life out of her like the time vampire that she knew it was.

Jill's hypochondria was back with a vengeance, too, getting the best of her by letting her believe she had aches because she caught Covid or had a bleeding ulcer due to all the bloating that she had been experiencing, as of late. All possible signs of menopause that she was clearly unaware of.

One day, she found herself hunched over her lover's dresser in a compromising position, doing a faceplant on the top of it with her head twisted sideways, as she huffed and puffed, tugging on the zipper at the back of a dress she had tried to squeeze into, but to no avail, and she so desperately had to take a fat dump.

She felt like Heidi Klum, out there, jumping around in a giant worm costume, on the red carpet at some costume party.

Suddenly the devil materialized as an air biscuit that flew straight out of Jill's ass, launching itself into mid-air before landing with a squishy splat on her shoulder, like a puck of

Carroll county cow dung, letting all the flies settle in on it as it began to sink into the center like a melting chocolate lava cake. It was stinking up the room.

The Devil had come to mess with her mind again. She had tried so hard to ignore that dark angel. There were warning signs of depression all around and she knew it after she had wasted days binge watching RHOA again, feasting her eyes on multiple season finales as she dreamed of escaping her own mind by becoming instantly wealthy overnight.

She was knee-deep in her favorite flavor of Halo ice cream, because she was fresh out of Ben & Jerry's, when she got a message from some random dude asking her how much she would charge to write stand-up for an upcoming holiday show he was headlining.

Jill was both intrigued and flattered, to say the least, that a man would ask her to write material for him. *This has never happened before in the history of comedy.*

She took him up on the offer once she found out that he also wanted her to write monster jokes, for Halloween, which she thought might be super silly AND fun to do.

Jill sat down and began to compose the first joke.

> "Two Doppelgangers
> plan a date
> One shapeshifter says
> to the other shapeshifter
> Let's hang out in person
> the other one says GREAT!
> You pick the person."

Jill thought the joke was funny but then she spontaneously tore it from the pages of her notebook and threw it against the wall, to see if it would stick like spaghetti, but instead, it fell to the floor like a limp biscuit.

"You son of a bitch! No. Not today, Satan!" She screamed in frustration, tugging at her hair as she lashed out in anger, with fire in her eyes, for no apparent reason. She could feel another hot flash creeping in.

It was only after hours of pacing back and forth across the marbleized floors in the kitchen, that she came to understand that, for whatever reason, there were times when she could not control her own demons, and there were times when she could not write. She knew she had to let go and stop fighting the forces that seemed to be controlling her mind at that moment, but she felt totally defeated.

* * *

"THIS IS THE DEVIL, BITCH!"

She heard that voice as she drifted off to la la land or, in her case, the land of the never-living nightmare. She was running from something but it just kept finding her in her dreams, no matter where she tried to hide or how fast she ran.

"DID YOU HEAR ME, BITCH? AM I COMING IN LOUD AND CLEAR OR SHALL I GIFT YOU WITH A CASE OF RINGING IN THE EARS UNTIL I GET YOUR FULL AND UNDIVIDED ATTENTION?" The devil asked. "FOR WHOM THE BELL TOLLS." The devil screamed in her ear.

"I have come to fill you with your daily dose of worthlessness so that you can get the fuck up and feel like holy hell all day long while other people say to you, 'good morning sunshine,' as they twirl around your waste of space ass with brightly colored coffee cups always half full, taunting you to take them down with all your might as you yank on their perfect tresses, ripping them off the pedestals they are perched upon, throwing them to the floor, tearing them down like the artist that you are, living wild out here in this concrete jungle with no hope for a future in sight."

Jill could not sleep and she was running out of food again fast. She had no money left on her online account to buy more with. She was frantically loafing around his condo, rummaging through cabinets, in search of substance. She'd even eaten her way through all the dry breakfast cereals. Luckily, she discovered a can of alphabet soup rolling around in the bottom of her Trader Joe's pickles tote. Then, all of a sudden, there came a loud rapping at the door.

Who the hell is that? I am not expecting a soul. Has someone come to kick me out? Could it be Max's wife? Did she finally figure out what dirty tricks he had up his sleeves and now she had come to call on his mistress like some crazy bitch-from-hell Karen character, straight out of Goodfellas, a woman who was going to push all of her buttons until she lost her fucking mind? I really should have asked more questions before I just straight-up moved into my lover's condo. But then again, I promised to follow my heart.

Jill crept across the carpet, quiet as a mouse. She slipped into her velvet slippers and slid across the slick bathroom tiles to grab the stool sitting next to the shitter.

When she climbed upon it, to raise herself up to the keyhole, she covered it first with one finger, just in case that Karen bitch had a gun and intended to shoot her eye out.

But much to Jill's surprise, there was nobody there that wanted to kill her. There was no one standing outside the door and the sight of the void caused her mind to flip out, running wild with ideas, wondering if the other woman was hiding behind the wall, in the halls, wielding an ax, out for revenge and fully ready to take her ass out.

Okay, Jill. Just be brave and breathe easy. After three deep breaths, she slid the chain into the locking position on the door, opening it just a crack so that she could peak out. Instead of the other woman on the other side, what Jill found were bags filled with fresh groceries from the local farmer's market, sitting outside the door.

She cautiously looked both ways before dragging that grocery store hall inside to have a look-see. At the bottom of one of the bags, she found a lovely gold, silver, and bronze foil Hallmark card. Enclosed it simply said: 'Stop eating garbage and go outside,' instantly making Jill grin cheek to cheek because she knew it was from Shantay and, for the first time in a long time, she felt like someone actually gave a shit about her again.

WINDY CITY WOMAN

Jill cooked herself a healthy meal and took a stroll down River East, near the Ogden slip, walking past the restaurants and art galleries that lined the long path along the canal.

Afterward, she and Shantay made their way over to Rumba together to grab the perfect cup of Metric coffee, topped off with that creamy, whipped, foamy heart of goodness that Jill had come to expect from her favorite coffee shop. It was the one place that she frequented the most often, as she had spent much of her time there, writing comedy and telling silly jokes to the staff because she liked to make people laugh.

Jill was seated in the picture window with Shantay. They were perched up high, on matching stools, swinging their legs around, in a playful way, while people-watching, when Shantay decided to get real with Jill by asking her straight up, "Is your sugar daddy the only source of income that you have?"

Jill paused for a moment to think of a lie before she responded to the awkward question. "Look, Shantay, it's like I told you before. I do work, okay?"

"Okay…So, how much money do you have saved from doing this work that you do? I mean, like actual, real money, in the bank? Don't worry, I'll wait…" Shantay slowly sat back, sipping on her coffee without a care in the world, as she waited for Jill to respond to her prying question.

"Some," Jill muttered. "Some is better than none."

"Come again?" Shantay asked.

"I have some saved, I said." Jill shifted in her seat, fussing incessantly over the silk scarf she had fashioned in a bow around her neck. She had been twirling it around her fingers, pulling it tighter and tighter, until the skin beneath it began to crepe together, blushing under the pressure that she was putting on the noose around her neck.

"Well, whatever sum you say it is, it certainly does not sound like enough to sustain you, if there were to be a real shit hits the fan situation...excuse me, may I?" Shantay quickly reached out to release the noose that Jill was twisting tightly. "Honey, you have got to learn to relax, or this city is going to eat you alive, just like it did last time you came here and went running home to mommy, remember?"

"I don't want to talk about the past, Shantay." Jill cut her off.

"And we don't have to. Look, all I know is that I really don't want to lose another friend to the burbs, where all the Chicago expats go to become boring people and die."

"So, you consider me a friend?" Jill smiled.

"I do." Shantay smiled back. "You make me laugh. I like your vibe, I feel like I can trust you, and I can relate to your hustle. I think there is a lot we can learn from each other. And besides, I could show you parts of this city that you have never seen before. I do own a car you know."

"No shit, really?"

"Yeah, really."

"Wow, I am so happy to have such a cool friend. I always wanted to have a friend who had my back." Jill said.

"And, furthermore..."

"Furthermore!" Jill played along.

"I truly believe that who we think we are now, is not who we are going to be in the future, you know what I mean? People like us, Pisces, we are fluid. We don't remain the same. We grow in waves. You and I, we are both trying to level up. We are both trying to get our foot in that revolving door. We are both fighting to remain relevant at this stage in our life. Only, there can be no shame in this game, no regrets, just respect, remember."

"Back up plans? No regrets? I like the way you think, Shantay! Always one step ahead of the game. Exactly the kind of friend that I need!" Jill complimented Shantay. "The kind that is going to help me rise above and level up."

"Look, I am telling you right now, all you need to do is you and God will take care of the rest. It is that simple."

Jill was listening, with intention, as Shantay continued to speak.

"Really! And, another thing I know is that there are only two things you cannot outrun in this life Jill, and death may have the final say, but you can trust and believe that there have been years that have just blown by my ass, where I have paid like zero dollars in taxes, and I should have, for real, because problems like back taxes just don't go away someday. They fester in the sun, like rotting garbage, until they stink like a dream that never came true. I consider myself an ally to all women." Shantay proclaimed before she let her voice take on a more somber tone, and she started to get real serious about what she was saying.

"I want to see all women get their due someday. And any man who tries to hold you back, or is trying to hide you or shame you, or who does not inspire the very best in you, or who is trying to bring you down, or who does not stand up for you, does not deserve your time or attention because they are garbage. And here is what I think, Jill. I think it is time for women everywhere to start taking out the trash!

We are not the ones inciting and incentivising violence. We are not the ones out there starting senseless wars.

War is dumb!

We are not the ones trying to solve problems with irreversible solutions, we do not murder *en masse..* We are not the ones using our fists to solve problems" she said, "and I do not ever need to repeat this for the problem to be a real one and I think it is about time for a change and I can feel one coming, I really can."

No sooner had she spoken those words, which required a moment of deep reflection, when a tall spender, fit woman, with hair like Dianna Ross, climbed down off the back of a city garbage truck, wearing a blue jumper and a pair of neon rain boots.

She was demanding that the driver stop the truck and back up so she could drag a can off the street corner to toss it into the back of the garbage truck that she was holding on to before the truck took off heading west, into the heart of the city, by way of Grand Avenue.

"I am on YOUR side Jill. I am not trying to shame or belittle you for what you do or how you make your money. That is not my function. I consider you a victim of your circumstances, much like many other women who have no real power…at least not yet.

I have been watching how you roll and I can totally tell that you have the ability to make bank if you want to and unlike some of these other no-talent basics, I actually want to see you prosper and get your due respect. Because, in my opinion, we women are owed that much from men who have had this power shift coming for a long time, trust me.

We grew up in the 70s. We saw what went on when men tried to normalize beating the shit out of their queens, as long as both parties were discreet and kept their mouths shut about it. I think women need to stick together, and always have a game plan, so they can keep it pushing when something goes wrong in their life so they don't end up like one of them dried up, desperate old cougars shaking that ass to the tune of ring my bell at the Red Head Piano Bar when all the old men are over there chasing fresh tail on Rush, if you get my drift."

She warned Jill, "Look, I am telling you, all I know for sure is the shit that I have seen with my own eyes and I have seen it happen many times, trust me. I have seen men throw out away all kinds of lovers here, and especially the aging ones, and they will do it without warning, too.

Suddenly, one day, your key fob simply does not work anymore and then you are locked out of the building and the life you thought you made for yourself, with no rights or access to your personal belongings, or your pets, while they freeze you out, and these men think nothing of it. They are not angels, Jill. Trust me, they are something much much darker."

"Oh, I don't think Max would ever do a thing like that!" Jill shook her head in denial.

"Oh Really?" Shantay rolled her eyes in sheer dismay. "Because they will build you up, tear you down, and ice you out in the blink of an eye. It is a pattern, a cycle of abuse. It is not the physical abuse that our mothers endured but it is a form of abuse, nonetheless, because it leaves you neglected and hopeless, with no voice and fighting to pick up the broken pieces of your heart and there is nothing that I can do to help any of those lost souls because the truth is that most of them do not belong in the big city anyways, but I think you are different. I think you do. I do think you actually belong here Jill. You have an edge. You are sharp."

"Really? Wow! That is fierce!" Jill placed her hands over her heart. "Thank You for saying so and I really mean it!"

"Well, you do keep coming back, as if you were a glutton

for punishment, which must mean that you are drawn to this place for a reason." Shantay pointed out. "I must admit, it is magnetic."

"Oh, wow, I guess you are right!" Jill found herself agreeing with everything Shantay had to say, as if the woman were preaching to the choir.

"You know, you are making me feel super motivated to get my shit together right away, and a little uneasy about the process at the same time," Jill confessed to Shantay as she began wringing her hands together in her lap, laughing nervously at the very suggestion that her fabulous life could end in a New York minute and without any warning.

Shantay reached over to place one of her hands over the top of Jill's, letting her appropriately pre-grieve the loss of a lifestyle that she hoped would last a lifetime. "Laugh now, cry later…"

Shantay continued to reveal her own choose-your-own-adventure scenarios to Jill, presenting her with a glimpse of her own future if she did not start to get her ass in motion and come up with a game plan, so that she could survive, on her own and without a man.

"Rich men forget about women much younger than you a hell of a lot sooner than he has, so consider yourself one of the lucky leftovers." she said. "He had you for lunch, twice, Yes, but will ice you out for all kinds of ridiculous reasons, by the same token. You gained five pounds, you seem neurotic, you ask too many questions, you want to meet the family, you text too often, you become needy as fuck, you are greedy as fuck, you disrespect them somehow, you will not go along with their idea of a good time, you no longer look good on their arm. There is always someone younger and more beautiful than you, in the city, and there always will be. So, what is your plan B?

And this entire time he has you believing that you are his

only dish, please. You need to learn to serve that shit up to him on a cold plate Jill, cold as ice…unless, of course. Do you want to couch surf for the rest of your life or do you want some real power before he reduces that walk-in closet, that he loaned you, into a dirty bucket overflowing with handouts, on the floor of some group home somewhere or some random homeless shelter that you stumbled upon in your latest stoned and drunken stupor."

"Oh Jesus, that sounds so insane and chaotic. Please talk less." Jill pleaded with Shantay to back down but she would not.

"You do not want to be the mistress forever, trust me. The other woman never gets half, always remember that." She warned.

"I know." Jill let out a great sigh, in total desperation, because she was completely overwhelmed.

"What you need to be is a bigger player than those ladies who are just looking to take on the role of that hot trophy wife. So that, in the end, they are the only ones left out here hustling because you used your brain a long time ago, by actually working for a living, by actually using your knowledge of the world to make it a better place…If you can pick up on what I am putting down."

"Oh, I picked it up." Jill was agreeable because she did not want to wind up ass out, and alone, broke and out of her mind, running the streets of Chicago.

"So tell me, how much do you charge for this writing work that you do?" Shantay asks Jill outright.

"Charge? I charge them for whatever it is that I want to buy with the money. I am currently elevating my wardrobe to the next level. I have turned my hard work into fashion and it is fabulous!" Jill proclaimed.

"Oh wow! You cannot be serious!" Shantay shook her head.

"Really, no joke." Jill sipped on her espresso with one pinky finger elevated high in the air, like some fancy hoity-toity heiress.

"And they pay you whatever you charge them?" Shantay asked, astounded.

"Well, within reason, I'm sure." Jill explained.

"Well, you must have found some rich-ass clients or something, damn! But then again..you do live in the right zip code to pick up that kind of work, plus you are funny, and creative so this is all starting to make more sense to me now. Maybe you were born to entertain, but you just haven't learned how to dance yet."

"What is THAT supposed to mean?" This statement piqued Jill's curiosity.

"It means you need to learn to take your craft or your talent more seriously and stop treating this job like a side hustle, if you want to survive in the city maybe start thinking about your future, you know?"

"Yes, Mother!" Jill joked

"No Jill. I really mean it. I think what you need is a financial manager or personal assistant or someone to help keep track of your appointments, deadlines, and expenses to help keep you goal oriented and more organized."

"An assistant? That sounds interesting. I have never thought about hiring an assistant before. That sounds like something rich people do."

"Exactly! This is why you need to strike while the iron is still hot and your lover is still paying your expenses. Get an assistant now, before he throws you out on the streets to fend for yourself because nobody is going to be your personal assistant if you are homeless, without resources, and on your ass honey." Shantay clarified. "I am just saying. You need to reign in your finances while there is still time to do so and start making a budget for yourself so that you are aware of what all of your expenses are, and start paying quarterly taxes, and all that business like shit. Are you holding on to receipts for all the business expenses you have so far, like that wardrobe that you may want to take a tax write off for because style, in your case, is part of the cost of doing business, as an entertainer."

"Receipts?" Jill scratched her head hard. "Oh, don't be silly. There is no proof that I am being paid to write anything. They just Venmo me money online and I spend it, so it is really more like bartering, than anything else, you know: trading goods for services.

"Jill, I know what trading goods for services means." Shantay just sat there shaking her head back and forth as Jill tried to explain how she was running a prosperous ghostwriting business when, in fact, she was doing no such thing.

"Say...I know Shantay...I have a great idea! You could be my personal assistant! I could pay you."

"Oh, no thank you honey. And besides, I think I bank more at my side hustle than you could afford to pay me."

"Really, you do?" Jill wanted to know more but her friend cut her off.

"Back to my point..." Shantay continued. "A personal assistant would take a certain amount of this burden off your shoulders is all I am saying. You will need to set up a business bank account as well. No, scratch that, you need to set up any bank account period, at any local bank. In fact, do what I do and get one local account, and then set up a bank account with an internationally recognized name, like Chase, so that, in case there is a SHTF situation, you will be able to ghost this town lickety-split."

"Great idea!" Jill agreed.

"I mean, do you even know if this sugar daddy of yours happens to be married or not?" Shantay wanted to know.

"He never talks about stuff like that but I do know he has had other serious girlfriends in the past. I don't really know what his situation is now because he lives a completely different life, in the big apple, and he is relatively secretive about everything, but then again, he has always been a man of mystery."

"Well, mystery usually has a middle name and it's called 'Another Woman' so you will still need a solid plan B in case his plan A comes to try and take you out. You do not understand the games these high-dollar executive types are capable of playing with all the shenanigans that go on among the one percent. They are capable of vanishing you too, you know." She warned Jill. "I mean, you have heard of Epstein Island, right? The last thing they want is to EVER be exposed."

"Oh my God! You may be right. I guess I will start looking for an assistant right away. Thanks for the pep talk because I really needed that swift kick in the pants!"

* * *

Jill felt super motivated about getting her financial house in order by thinking about hiring an assistant the very next day. She found it curious that she suddenly had the ability to focus on a task worth doing well, for once. She was starting to feel motivated again, but she did not want to push her luck, because her hot flashes were likely to return, but she had been noticing that they had become fewer and further between, lately, which she counted as a blessing by itself.

She was trying to decide if she wanted to hire an assistant, in real life, which seemed expensive and time-consuming, to say the least, or maybe just hire a virtual one – like an Alexa. Like a robot that she could turn on and off with the flip of a switch. An IT that was at her beck and call like some kind of A.I. masterpiece of a fake person with major business skills, that could just kiss your ass and make money all day.

However, a virtual assistant cannot make coffee for you, or listen to you bitch and moan about your clients over coffee. She considered the finer points of an android as she began to imagine what it might be like to interview a personal assistant in real life.

Perhaps she could find someone cool to bounce ideas off of and tell jokes to. Maybe they would become fast friends. Maybe she would be from a modern generation and help Jill fix all of the fucked up issues that she was having with all this recent technology she was forced to use in order to communicate with an isolated world gone mad.

And, was it *she* or *they* now? What exactly IS the proper pronoun for generation next and was she using their pronouns in the correct way? Suddenly she felt old and completely out of touch.

She impatiently waited, for what seemed like forever, for a candidate to respond to her inquiry about hiring an assistant in real life.

She had guessed this was due to so many people being sick because of the pandemic but she could not be certain. Then, one day, lo and behold, she saw that she had a response to a job post that she had placed on LinkedIn.

This response was followed up by a vanilla envelope, which Jill received via snail mail, that contained this applicant's resume and the most impressive handwritten cover letter, list of credentials, and personal references, that Jill had ever laid eyes on in her whole life. It read like a menu at some high dollar restaurant downtown, as it was formatted in such an eye-catching way and composed with such attention to detail.

Jill immediately set up an interview with Gretchen Elizabeth Piper who she jokingly would refer to as Von So-and-So, in private. She had completely bypassed her own game plan to schedule a meeting with each candidate, via Zoom, prior to meeting with them in real time.

Jill was already running a few minutes late for the interview she had scheduled with Von So-and-So and so she decided to pop into the bakery next door to the place where she had arranged to meet with her, in order to pick up a few festive pastries to munch on, in case they wanted to grab coffee or bubble tea before, during, or after their little pow wow.

As Jill waited to be served, she ignored a text from Von So-and-So that asked where are you because the lady behind the counter, at the donuts shop, was busy asking her what kind of cake pops she wanted to go along with the pink glazed donuts that she had picked out.

Jill watched the super sweet lady place the sprinkled goodies in the pretty box she had folded to hold them, as she daydreamed about how she planned to hire Von So-and-So on the spot if they hit it off because she had not bothered to set up any other interviews.

When Jill finally walked into the coffee shop, she immediately spotted her applicant, based on the LinkedIn photo she saw of her.

Von So-and-So was sucking in all the fat from the buccal region on her face, revealing a jagged pair of ultra-razor-sharp high cheekbones, that were unmistakably European, as Jill approached her carrying that box of goodies.

"Would you like a donut?" Jill suggested as she opened the pink box to reveal the selection as she offered Von So-and-So a cheerful hello.

"I do not eat donuts and garbage. I am no longer a child." Von So-and-So proclaimed, opening her astonishing mouth to reveal a jagged row of Chiclets-style vampire teeth that could rival Sookie Stackhouse's fangs in any blood-sucking vampire thriller.

"Wow, you really *are* a firecracker. Get it?" Jill tilted down the top of the pastry box to reveal the name of the pastry shop she just came from. It was printed on the top of it, as Von So-and-So rolled her eyes, letting out a long, deep sigh, like a deflated debutante.

"Take a seat boomer," Von So-and-So insisted with a total sense of entitlement.

Jill did not want to correct Von So-and-So for making an error in judgment by mislabeling her generation because she did not want to embarrass the zoomer but she had made the mistake of sitting a little too close to the humorless bitch and the next thing she knew Von So-and-So was shoving her out of the way to yanked her stuck scarf out from under Jill's sizable caboose.

"I trust you found my papers in order," Von So-and-So said as she abruptly stood, in a huff, to relocate herself to the furthest point on the circular booth, re-arranging her accouterments, such as pen and paper, as she sat impatiently, tapping on her crystal-clear, shatterproof, glass thermos, filled with freshly pumped sparkling water and a few bitter wedges of lime.

"Oh yes, I did. Thank you so much for sending it to me. I was so impressed with all your experience and references! So, tell me, Von So-and-So, what do you believe is the key thing that qualifies you for this position as my new assistant?"

"I have a PhD in reality, unlike yourself. And clearly, you are in need of this 'assistance' that you speak of." Von So-and-So said, making air quotes while donning what appeared to be a very forced Cheshire Cat kind of smile.

"Are you a Domme?" Jill asked her. "I mean, I am just curious. You may want to look into that whole S & M lifestyle because something tells me that you don't pull any punches.

You know, I get a hell of a lot of men hitting me up on Tinder and Match who truly want a woman like you to punish them, but I'm just too old for all that role playing anymore."

"I know." Von So-and-So agreed with sad eyes.

"I mean, I'm in menopause for Christ's sake and they want me to wear a black balloon costume and beat them into submission? I mean, come on! I say, get the fuck out of here with that!"

"Silence!" Von So-and-So slammed her fist down hard on the metal table that was bolted to the floor in front of them. "I am not here to make small talk and I must insist that you provide me with the job description that I requested immediately! I will give you 24 hours to procure this document. I need to know exactly what I can expect if I choose to take this position, so that I can make an informed decision about my future and plan my free time." She stood up with perfect posture.

"Okay, fair enough. I think we are vibing here, don't you? I can certainly write a job description for you to review."

"If I find the terms of this document to be agreeable, I will then sign off on it and return it to you promptly with any necessary revisions. I trust that we will remain in touch." Von So-and-So said. "Good day," and then she walked away.

* * *

When Jill woke up from her latest food coma, she realized that after getting drunk and oversleeping her alarm again that she now had only a limited amount of time left to create a job description for Von So-and-So.

She was not even certain what she had written when she

sent off the job description for her assistant's approval, but she was pleased as punch when Von So-and-So accepted the job offer to become her personal assistant, 'once they worked out their differences.'

These differences, however, were more stark than Jill had expected.

Whenever she asked her new assistant to do something for her, Von So-and-So would whip out a hard copy of her laminated job description to prove to Jill that she was not being paid to do whatever it was that the boss wanted her to do. So Jill strongly suspected that Von So-and-So was actually trying to 'quiet quit' on her from the word go.

But it came to a head when Jill approached Von So-and-So one afternoon to have a heart-to-heart conversation with her about a shoe box filled with receipts that she had meant to include in the tax items she was supposed to give to her. She had just realized she had accidentally thrown the box down the trash shoot along with all of those high-end shopping bags that had been collecting in the corners of her lover's condo since the day she started shopping.

Jill could tell that Von So-and-So could tell that she had been crying when she approached her to explain what had happened to that box of receipts but Von So-and-So did not seem to care at all. She did not even bother to ask the sad artist what was the matter. So Jill droned on forever, pouring her heart out to Von So-and-So over sad love stories that the numbers wizard seemed not the least bit keen on listening to.

"You need a therapist." Von So-and-So stated emphatically. She was showing that she was serious, when she made this statement, as she crossed both her arms and legs over each other to protect her own set boundaries because she knew that Jill had none. "Playing therapist is not part of my job description."

PAINTED BLACK

Jill was scratching her head in disbelief about how that little Gen Zoomer Von-So-and-So had the nerve to tell her she needed therapy, and right to her face, in fact.

She clearly has a major stick up her ass. Jill thought but then after she polished off a bottle of Grey Goose mixed with candy corn-colored jello shots, because she heard someplace that collagen was great for your skin, she concluded that Von So-and-So might actually be right.

She finally broke down and decided to get in touch with a local shrink, someone in walking distance, because she did sort of feel like she was losing her noodle. Plus, the holidays were quickly approaching and Jill knew that was, by far, the most depressing time of the year for her. She had no fond memories of any month that ended in the letters E and R like ever.

"Fuck! Life sucks!" Jill cried out loud, as she threw a glass ashtray against the wall, when she realized how depressed she had been over every holiday for practically her entire life, or for at least as far back as she could remember.

As a child she had lived as a latch key kid in poverty. Her mother could only afford the kind of Christmas tree where the needles fell off after a few weeks. The kind where the bark always looked like it had the ich, like some sick fish, with the way its dry brown skin would peel off the second you tried to cram it down in the Christmas tree stand. Just another bald Charlie Brown-type Christmas tree, in another sad house, on another sad gray snowy day, along some depressing street. The occasion had been marked by some frenetic jazz music and dirty children, frolicking and acting grateful for what they had as if they were the lucky ones for no logical reason whatsoever.

Jill did her best to focus on letting go of that dystopian nightmare of a past as she had practiced the art of compartmentalization, for most of her life, much in the same way that pirates conceal hidden treasure in a buried chest: by wrapping it up in chains, and chucking it overboard where it would be lost at sea with the key, missing in action, forevermore.

Jill's instinct was always to escape from the world outside and hide in bed because it was the only place where she felt even remotely safe, the place where she went to escape when the shit hit the fan, instead of facing the facts of life.

A place where she could quiet her mind without thinking about the truth for a while. *She was thinking back to a time in her childhood when her mother never believed a word that ever came out of her mouth and now she was a fiction writer.* And the irony that was her life. *Maybe the new therapist will teach me some coping mechanisms to deal with all the devil,* Jill thought as she upgraded her tent to a fortress, complete with a canopy of colored lights, where she nested with her Dream, surrounded by oversized pillows in various shades of blood red and glittering gold.

With her laptop balancing on her knee, Jill went on Google Maps to find a therapist close by her. That is when she came across a woman with the most curious name that she had ever heard in her entire life: Persephone Ultima.

"Wow, what a name, Dream!" Jill read it aloud to her cat, over and over again, as if this therapist had become another character in Jill's fictitious life.

Jill had hoped that she could connect with this new therapist via Telehealth or via Zoom, as she had no desire to get all bundled up in her snow pants, to walk along the cold-as-fuck lakefront to meet with this person, in person.

Persephone Ultima did not accept Zoom calls and

furthermore, she insisted on meeting in person.

Jill found it odd and somewhat mysterious that this woman only wanted to meet face to face, given that the pandemic was still raging and long Covid was becoming a real concern. But instead of arguing this point, Jill just went along with the program the therapist put in place for her.

Jill preferred working with a female therapist because they had a vagina which was something Jill could relate to.

She had burned her way through so many female therapists, over the years, ever since she had been diagnosed, with clinical depression and high anxiety, in her early twenties. Not that they, or any of the medications she ever took for the conditions, ever resolved any of her issues.

But really, who is counting therapists anymore? Aren't I supposed to be considered the brave one just for asking for all of this help in the first place?

She muttered under her boozy breath before scheduling an intake appointment with Persephone. After that, she cried herself to sleep in her glamping worthy cocoon.

* * *

Jill tried to cancel her appointment with Persephone on the day that it was due to take place because she felt too lazy and cold to get all bundled up and walk outside, dodging the falling icicles dangling down from tall buildings, like shards of glass, gleaming as they dripped in the sun, waiting to stab her in the heart as she made her way down LSD, facing the whipping wind, to walk to her therapist's office.

Jill was getting ready to leave a voicemail when Persephone picked up her call.

"Don't you have a receptionist to answer your calls?"

Jill was fishing for a legitimate reason to cancel her appointment, but she could not think that fast first thing in the morning.

She was trying to call her therapist out for being a cheap ass phony baloney, when Persephone spoke sweetly by saying,

"Oh, don't be silly. It is too late to cancel now, without paying in full, since all cancellations made, according to my website, for any reason whatsoever, required at least a 24-hour notification, which Jill had not provided."

So instead, Jill dragged her ass out of the bed and got bundled up to brave the elements. Persephone had insisted that Jill push through the day to meet her in person and Jill came to learn pretty fast that Persephone was a pushy woman with ways, who always seemed to have the last word about everything.

Her office was filled with some wacky, scary-ass tribal art that made Jill's skin crawl and gave her the heebie-jeebies on top of her already inherent anxieties and plethora of phobias.

Jill was starting to wonder if she had taken a wrong turn somewhere and wound up at the Chicago Torture Museum somehow. She did a double take to look at some wicker monkey trash basket that was squatting in the corner of the room, across from the place where she stood, with its legs spread akimbo to accommodate the waste can and its tongue hanging out as it stared up at her with its piss-yellow eyes like some a Jeffrey Dahmer nightmare.

Jill was starting to question if she was in the right place until, moments later, she happened to notice the shrink's last name, spelled backward, in black paint, across the frosted glass window that hung from a rusted industrial chain that dangled above the doorway she had passed through.

Jill sat down on the only chair in the cavernous room. The

antique seat had a dusty, embroidered seat cushion and when she sat upon it, it exploded into a smoke cloud, filled with God only knows what kind of poisonous toxins.

Boy, was Jill glad that she had come prepared with her N95 mask that day! When the cloud settled, she looked up only to come face to face with a black painting that was hanging on the wall directly above the monkey that she had spotted earlier.

The painting was a night scene, a starless night, with a giant creature lurking in the shadows, hunched over the frame as if he was attempting to squeeze himself into a cannibal selfie, with his barbaric beady little eyes ablaze. He appeared to be violently chewing on the arm of a living human being with his great, gaping, ghost-bird of a mouth, after he already polished off the other arm, as his main course, before Jill had arrived in that frightening place. This cannibal looked menacing but he really had no discernible nut sack, or any kind of frankfurter of his own for matter. She told herself not to dwell on it but she could not look away.

Before she could finish her insane art critique, Persephone made a grand entrance into that room to usher Jill down a long shotgun shaped corridor, covered in layers and layers of peeling paint—like the halls of the Mansfield reformatory back in Ohio.

Persephone was dragging her captive audience deeper and deeper, into the belly of that beast of that building, until they reached a dead end, where they entered a room, which was painted black and seemed to defy all laws of space and sound as Jill became increasingly disoriented in that cave like dwelling.

"What the hell is this place?" Jill asked in fear.

"Exactly." said Persephone

"Exactly what?" Jill clutched at her throat because she was having a hard time breathing after she was attacked by that thick dust that now clung to her face like those little metal pieces that you drag onto some clown in this kid game, the name of which, at the moment, completely escaped her mind.

Instead of responding to Jill's question, Persephone had simply vanished, only to reappear seated under a naked light bulb screwed into a metal platter ring that was dangling down in the middle of that very dark space as if it were an interrogation room.

Persephone immediately started pounding away on this old-school typewriter, that was perched on the desk above the Herman Miller chair she was seated in with her white, horn-rimmed glasses propped smartly on the bridge of the Meryl Streep nose as she gazed at Jill who took a seat in the only other chair in the room. The one that was positioned directly within her hawkish line of sight.

Persephone started their intake session abruptly at the top of the hour. She proceeded without warning. The intake lasted exactly 55 minutes, on the dot, during which time the therapist asked Jill a litany of rapid-fire questions about herself, one after another, without giving her any time to consider the consequences of her answers before moving on to the next question, like a quiz.

The first few questions were simple for Jill to answer because everyone always asked these questions everywhere you went and almost every day. In fact, Jill was impressed with her own ability to recall the answers to these questions so quickly.

When the questions became more personal in nature, Jill began to slow down. She had a tougher time answering them because they were of such a personal nature so her answers required more thought.

She knew that if she was to insinuate, in any way, that she may be, in fact, any kind of danger to herself or others, she knew that she could be locked up in a psych ward on a 51/50 hold after being pink-slipped for a 72-hour observation because she had been there and done that.

So when Persephone asked Jill, "What is your relationship like with your mother?" instead of blurting out the completely justified response like 'She is dead to me,' Jill held her tongue in order to carefully consider her response but, before she had figured out the proper way to answer, Persephone simply stated, out loud, while typing that,

"Jill is hesitant to address this topic and prefers to move on to the meat of the matter, in order to address more pressing issues that are at the very core of what has brought her here today to seek out my professional knowledge."

Jill was laughing her ass off, on the inside, as she listened to Persephone weaving her own narcissistic narrative, responding to every question on Jill's behalf, as she proceeded to pound her words out feverishly on that super fly, wood-paneled, retro approved typewriter —which was a total blast from the past— sitting there as if she were competing in a speed typing contest as her long crimson nails banged away at that thing.

Jill could not believe that this woman was simply making shit up, about her life, as she went along. *I mean, is this a joke or something?* She thought.

"What is your occupation?" was the final question on the intake questionnaire that Persephone was filling in, on her behalf.

"I write fiction. I make shit up for a living, that is what I do." Jill confessed, with a certain appreciation for the irony of that statement again as she burst out in laughter.

However, her laughter soon turned to tears as she said.
"My mother never believed anything that I ever told her." Jill confessed to Persephone as she grabbed a Kleenex from the box that the therapist held out.

"I'm afraid that that's our time. The time is up." Persephone soon said.

Jill actually considered it quite refreshing that she should find such a unique therapist. One who was letting her off the hook so easily in therapy.

Persephone was the first one to just skip over any area of her life that she did not want to talk about, so naturally Jill scheduled a follow-up appointment for the next week just to have someone to talk to.

The next day Jill arranged for Von So-and-So to stop over for a powwow and in order to discuss a bunch of trivial shit that the comedy writer had on her mind, which apparently had her Gen Z assistant triggered in a big way when she went off on Jill, yet again, only this time by accusing her of being a time sucking vampire.

Well, she is right, to a point. Jill laughed off the comment.

The first part of Jill's meeting with Von So-and-So went off without a hitch, given that the meeting was at Max's place, which meant that Jill could not be late.

Von So-and-So showed up on time as always, with her carbonated water and hard-boiled eggs, as she munched on her Muesli mix, out of a mason jar—which made it sound like she was crushing gravel with her incisors as she spoke in her thick and commanding German accent.

Jill was considering how Von So-and-So would make an excellent character for the next stand-up set she wrote about 'The Gen Z woke assistant from hell' when Von So-and-So cleared her throat to ask a question.

"Did you find a therapist?"

"Well, sort of..." Jill answered.

"What is that supposed to mean?" Von So-and-So wasn't joking.

"Oh, nothing, It's just that, I guess, I mean, I sort of found the entire experience to be, well, rather unsettling, to be honest."

"Really." Von So-and-So gave Jill that speak to the hand gesture she frequently used to silence the boss, shutting her down so she could make comments on the subject. "I do not need the play-by-play. I simply want to know if this task has been performed so that I may put a check mark next to that on my list." She made a swift upward sweeping motion, with her pen, in one of her many day-planners.

"Cross being the keyword in *that* sentence indeed!" Jill rolled her eyes right to heaven, in front of her assistant, who was hovering over her substantial day planner, white-knuckling a red pen as she feverishly moved from one task to the next in a swift and methodical motion that had Jill mesmerized into submission.

"Now then, shall we proceed to the next matter at hand?" Von So-and-So asked Jill, who had long ago checked out but had also given up on her secret plan to escape to the bathroom, to suck on the Sunday Brunch Sativa vape she wanted to sample.

Instead, Jill found herself sitting up a little straighter in her chair to mimic the postural moves of her stealthy assistant, who seemed to know exactly how precious time was as she tackled the last few bullet points on her to-do list, before wrapping up her meeting with the joker.

"Oh, by the way… How much do comedy writers in the city charge?"

"You mean, how much do I charge to write comedy for my clients?" Jill asked before she carefully answered. "Well, I guess it is based on a sliding fee scale, really."

"What the hell does this mean?" Von So-and-So seemed so serious.

"Well, you see…I let my sugar daddy take care of my basic needs so I can blow the extra money I make, writing comedy, on buying the bling I want in my life like Louis, Prada, Gucci, Fendi, frolic, pop them tags and so on and so forth. I don't want Max to think that I am a gold digger, after all. Hell, I'm the one over here still waiting for him to come home." She hung her head low as if in defeat.

"But you hardly ever see him, right?" Von So-and-So mentioned. "Anyways, what does it matter? Never mind. Try to remain focused please." Von So-and-So was rubbing her head with three of her fingers, and it looked as if she had a migraine coming on strong. "This makes no sense at all, from a business perspective," Von So-and-So observed.

"Why not? I think it does. I mean, I get the things I need from one place and the things I want, and would feel super guilty asking for, from another place. What is so hard to understand about that?"

"Look Jill, you hired me to put your financial house in order and that is exactly what I intend to do with my time, so that you no longer need to rely on a man to get by. This is not a joking matter, this is the rest of your life that we are talking about Jill and you are not getting any younger.

I need to know exactly how much we are able to charge for this comedy that you write, so that we can plan your financial future accordingly. And so, I will be devoting the rest of my time this week to researching exactly how much your comedy is worth. Good day." Von So-and-So capped her red pen and put it away in its designated pocket, next to the green pen that she used to mark Jill's money moves with.

Jill was still trying to talk to Von So-and-So as she was

dashing out the door, but to no avail. Later that same day, she received a voicemail from Von So-and-So, recapping their weekly meeting, like it was her job or something. She basically summed everything up by stating:

"Now is the time to plan your future wisely, Jill. You should be focused on gaining financial stability in the present so that, moving forward, you will have the confidence and peace of mind to know that your money is a safety net which is working for you in times of need, because you'll have invested wisely to gain the financial freedom that we all deserve to enjoy in our golden years of retirement."

Investments, the future, financial freedom, wow! She sounds like someone who just passed the series 7 to pitch junk stocks to suckers. Jill snickered under her breath as she listened to the message again while eating pumpkin pie and drinking Bourbon warm and straight from the bottle.

She really will accept nothing less than success, will she? That Von So-and-So Von So-and-So. Jill stuck her finger down her throat as she made a fake gagging gesture at Dream. *Von So-and-So is completely overqualified for this position, and perhaps it is advisable that she tender her resignation, effective immediately, given this current revelation.*

CRICKETS

Jill did not hear from Von So-and-So at all over the Christmas holiday. Instead, she spent her time writing stand-up; and talking on the phone to Twila, whose conversations had never amounted to anything more than an endless cascade of thoughtless ramblings which did not amount to a hill of beans.

"Oh Mylanta! Is that you Jill? I feel like we haven't talked in ages!" Twila pointed out as Jill fired up a joint, sat back, and closed her eyes to try and relax.

"So anywho, this gal down at the food bank gave us some expired food the other day. It's like they never check the date on that stuff, gee wiz! I am not eating expired meat again. It gives me the runs." She continued "And then they tried to pull a fast one on us by not listing the exp because they bag things in Ziplock and add the dates with a Sharpie themselves now, How cheap can you be? I mean, come on!"

Could Twila actually be one of those time vampires that Von So-and-So was always complaining about?

Jill listened to Twila who had unleashed, yet another lengthy monologue on her, the kind that was guaranteed to bore her to death again.

Jill was suddenly regretting that she had just shared with Twila that she had been feeling deeply depressed lately when her friend then used that subject as a launching pad to go off on some senseless speech about how she was depressed ever since thieves broke into her house and stole two of her seven Singer sewing machines, which no burglar in their right fucking mind would ever take, in the middle of a break-in, no matter how much they liked to sew, because they weigh more than a bag of hammers.

Jill got so sick and so tired of listening to Twila ramble on, about shit that she did not care about, when she finally decided that she could not take it any more so she asked, point blank and in a mighty huff, "Do you have anything of value to add to the conversation? Because I have shit to do today." Jill snapped.

"So, have you heard from your mom lately?" Twila asked. For Jill, that was the last straw because she was triggered.

"No, Twila. No, I have not. And why? Why? Because you want to know if she is still screwing my Dad? Is that it? It happened twice, alright, just let it go, GOD! Furthermore, do you really want to know what I think TWILA?" Jill added.

"Oh sure!" Twila seemed agreeable to constructive criticism.

"I think YOU, you need a therapist. There I said it, *that* is what I think!" Jill shouted into the phone before she hung up on Twila, vowing never to speak to her crusty old friend ever again.

Before she could take a deep breath, her phone rang. It was Von So-and-So, who apparently had been doing her market research. What she had discovered was that Jill could actually charge a mint selling stand-up comedy and nobody would say boo about it because the price was subjective, given that it was considered art.

"You see, Jill, if you play your cards right, you could make enough money, in less than a year, to purchase the condo you are currently standing in."

VON SO-AND-SO

Jill had decided to be a more productive version of herself as she began combing through the slew of emails that Von So-and-So had forwarded to her attention, regarding potential clients that she may want to consider writing for, in order to quickly reach her goal of being a first-time homeowner in Chicago.

Luckily, Von So-and-So had also provided Jill with an instructional email entitled READ THIS FIRST, in all caps. In the body of this email, she wrote, "Just remember, you do not need to tackle all of these clients at once. Just select the ones that you believe would be the best fit for you and I will take care of the rest."

Jill was eager to start writing but soon she became overwhelmed by the sheer volume of new clients that she had to select from.

Luckily, Von So-and-So had created a system to help Jill figure out how to determine who to select based on if they were offering her what Von So-and-So referred to as a 'do-able deadline,' meaning a deadline that Jill could reasonably make—given that she was not the fastest writer in the world and she often experienced certain setbacks due to her hot flash-induced ADHD and her spontaneous bouts of anxiety and depression, tied with her unwavering addiction to reality TV.

Jill had been so concerned that she was going to feel lonely and horrible over the holidays, but oddly enough, her loneliness evaporated into thin air as soon as she began creating characters for new comedians.

Jill was writing for women who wanted to join the circus, she was writing for smart women with tramp stamps and amazing powers of observation, who also happened to be secretly very funny people. She was writing for The divas, the dreamers, and the queens, and all those women who desperately wanted to be women or just to be seen. And she was writing for everybody in between.

First off, in that motley crew of misfits, there was Donna Sue, a small-town librarian from Hicksville Illinois, who worked part-time, as a barista downtown, where she would frequent all the local comedy clubs to participate in open mic nights every other Friday.

There was Charity, the traveling clown, who told jokes exclusively about the circus and how she would not work for peanuts. 'Look, let's get one thing straight, okay? I *am* Charity, I do not *work* for charity!' that was the slogan she had created for herself and then used, in the past, to kick off every single one of her sets.

So, she hired Jill to write new material for her when she started to feel like a one-hit wonder, after some heckler told her that she always did the same show and that she needed to get some new material or be tested for early onset Dementia or whatever the hell that was that just kept making her repeat herself all the time.

Jill helped her tweak her material and add more complexity to it, to help her extend the life of the act that she so desperately seemed to want to re-invent until the day her audience just could not stand to listen to talk any longer.

Sage was another new client that Von So-and-So drummed up. A local burlesque dancer-slash-stand-up comedian, who dwelled somewhere in river north and performed for only the richest of rich down on Rush Street, at some private club, in a top-secret underground location that was somewhere in the heart of the loop.

It operated much like a speakeasy, with a secret knock that only the VIP clients knew how to bang out as they pushed their eyeballs through the long crack in the door there to get a glimpse inside. Because, when the clock struck midnight, all the dirty little Dommes came out to play, cloaked in the most expensive and exquisite regalia and dripping in diamonds.

The speakeasy was more like a theatrical brothel, at best, filled with other private dancers, just like Sage, who were hanging around, for as long as they could, living on all the borrowed time they could afford while waiting for some rich millionaire, like Batman, to sweep them off their feet by throwing off some serious bat vibes before they escaped in his bat mobile, vanishing underground by way of lower Wacker drive.

SAGE ON STAGE

Sage introduced herself to the club members as Jill took a seat in the front row at her client's show.

"My name is Sage, NOT Summer, a/k/a, all the leaves are brown and the sky IS gray, NO bitch! Say my name and welcome to my least favorite season of them all...the holidays! Some of the busiest tourist days of all, and among the most profitable here as well.

"I have some comedy for you tonight." She announced. "because I like to see my customers both laugh AND cry. I guess you could say, I'm a sadist in that way." She laughed along with her many fans. This next bit is one I like to call *The tourist T shirt* and it comes with a parting gift so pay attention because you might win something." She winked at her fans playfully before she began her act.

> **THE TOURIST T SHIRT**
>
> "When you live in a REAL city
> and no I am not talking about
> Evanston, Skokie or
> some other boring burbs
> or one of the airports
> or any other place that is
> actually 45 minutes outside
> of the city which is also
> not the city
>
> What I am talking about
> is the kind of place
> you actually WANT to visit

like downtown Chicago
(pause) NOT Cleveland
or any other mistake by the lake
someone tried to call a real city once
just because THEY stay there

you can't hail a cab in Cleveland, can you?
Therefor that in NOT a real city

I am speaking of the kind of place
where you CAN actually
walk out on the street and hail
a fucking cab at the curb

you know, a real city, like Chicago!
A place where all the tourists
come to clown around downtown
forcing all the locals
to co-mingle with these obnoxious strangers
who can't see fit to leave their bad manners or
their moody ass fucking teenagers at home

You know they stand right on the bridge
to the loop now, across from River North
and they flip the bird at Trump tower
in every single selfie?

And their kids all suck
Like we want to look at their
resting ass bitch faces
while they are walk
around the streets
on a forced
family vacation.

With their roly-poly eyes rocking
back and forth in their sockets
dressed like something straight out

of a freak show with those Frankenstein pants
and Lu Lu Loser spider bras they sport
running around here half naked
with their arms crossed over their chests
acting awkward as fuck while the boys
are busy tripping over their shoe laces.

The CDC says the pandemic is over
So suddenly we have got
all of these tourists
coming out of the
woodwork, descending
on downtown family style
like they just stepped off
a double-decker tour bus
right in front of a Buca di Beppo

and you mean to tell me
all these out-of-towners
are magically immune
to Covid 19?

Like it's some Christmas miracle
or something
and in the meantime
they are multiplying by the thousands
descending on our home turf
in this concrete jungle
all dazed and confused as fuck
like something straight out of
a zombie apocalypse
searching for pigs in space
because they can't figure out
why all those amazing
skyscrapers they came to see
and take photos of
are now jamming up

they cell phone signals
so their google maps won't update instantly
and it is beyond obvious that they look like
they have zero clue what is going on
and these people are about to get robbed

And these tired ass zombie tourists
who are not used to getting exercise
by walking, they have no patience
roaming around lost and entitled
approach us Chicagoans
to ask us stupid ass questions
that they should already know
the answers too
like we work for the fucking
information desk over at
Bloomingdales

but I'm not bitter just vengeful which is why I recently created this new line of merchandise including these amazing T-shirts that I like to refer to as your First Line of Defense."

(The comedian walks over to a pile of t-shirts and holds one of them up to read it out loud to the audience)

"Okay, now these expressions range from polite to pissed off to postal."

(The comedian holds the first shirt up to read it)

**I DON'T KNOW
SO DON'T ASK**

(She read the second shirt)

DO I KNOW YOU?

(She reads the third shirt)

SCRAM!
GET LOST!
BEAT IT!

(She reads the fourth shirt)

SEND NUDES

(She reads the fifth shirt)

NOT TODAY, SATAN!

THE HOLY GHOSTS

"So, speaking of tourists,
One sunny day in Streeterville
I was picking up this
2-for-1 deal on eye drops
at the corner drugstore
cause I like to stay high
in the windy city
when this freaky family
who looked like some shit
straight off Seventh Heaven
waltzes into the Walgreens
dressed from head to toe
in their Sunday best
which was all white

So the father figure of this cult
approaches the counter
to inquire about his family
having their passport photos taken

and the associate was busy
trying not to laugh his fucking
ass off behind his loose fitting mask
before he managed to compose himself

> for long enough to explain
> to this mad man that you cannot
> wear all white to have passport photos taken
>
> I just stood there laughing
> my ass off too as I watched
> this entire shit show go down
>
> So the father manages to talk
> the associate into taking
> the passport photos anyways
> and the family left the white masks
> they were wearing on as well
> which just ends up looking like a bunch
> of ghosts with floating eyeballs hovering
> at different levels on a white backdrop
> It was the spookiest photo I had ever seen
>
> Hell, I even tried to encourage the heavenly father
> to consider purchasing a few of my tourist t-shirts
> to have their passport photos taken in
> but they just got spooked and drifted away."

***

Jill had been writing at a feverish pitch, in order to meet all her new deadlines, because she wanted to impress Von So-and-So, when suddenly her world came crashing down around her.

It happened when she was listening to this voicemail that Twila left. Twila had done the unforgivable, by mentioning Jill's mother's name several times, on the voice mail recording she had left her dear friend.

Hearing that name had triggered Jill to have an unpleasant memory about her past as she cursed Twila's name out loud, stewing in her unresolved PTSD.

Jesus, this woman really can't take a fucking hint, can she? She is so insensitive. really! I mean, my God, she is so obnoxious. At least we live in different states now so she can't just pop over here to bum a smoke off me any old time that she pleases anymore… that really used to burn my ass and drive me up the wall.

Jill tried to remain calm by thinking only positive thoughts. She did so by fondly reminiscing about how her conversations with her dear friend used to flow oh so naturally, as Twila always had her in stitches, telling funny stories about all the local yokels that she knew, ever since she was knee-high to a grasshopper.

But Twila had become nothing more than a chatterbox and a bore, who never had anything new to say because she never did much of anything. It was always just the same thing, in the same way, taking place on a different day out there in sticks in the middle of that forgotten land of soy fields that the rest of the country kindly referred to as 'the heart of it all.'

Jill bit down hard on her clenched fist until it began to sting and shake involuntarily under the weight of all the pressure that she felt that she was under.

"I may have to cut you out of my life!" She said as if she were speaking directly to Twila, who was somehow standing right in front of her. "I have outgrown you as my corn hole partner!" She proclaimed. "Thanks for the laughs but I no longer need you in my life!"

Jill was busy trying to light the wrong end of her cigarette, with her hands still shaking, as she continued to blindly obsess over the way that Twila had just poured salt into an old wound that never healed properly.

Jill knew this was not the past and that she had thrown out her roller skates and given up masturbating under the faucet in the family bathtub years ago but somehow she could still feel her heart beating out of her chest now, faster and faster, as if she was trapped in that nightmare all over again.

Suddenly she lost control as her breathing became shallow. She was experiencing chest pains. She was gasping for air when that cigarette, with its burnt filter, fell from her fingers scorching the carpet beneath her feet before she had the chance to stomp it out.

Jill clutched at her throat as she raced to the freezer gasping for air. She closed her eyes, as she forced herself to suck in the cold vapors from the ice box in order to breathe once again.

She deeply disliked the way those panic attacks would creep up on her in the most unexpected ways, debilitating her physically and leaving her so emotionally drained that she spent most of her time feeling as if she were drowning in air as if it were water.

She was just about to remove her head from the freezer when she noticed the Grey Goose chilling there that she had forgotten about long ago. She paused, momentarily, because she felt like she could not pass up the chance to day drink, pass out, and just forget about life for a while but then she spoke to herself in her own voice.

There is a time and a place for sleep but this time you are going to handle this trigger like an adult before you end up out on your ass, drunk and homeless.

Jill slammed the freezer door shut, choosing to walk away from that bottle for the first time in a long time, choosing instead to focus on writing an email to her assistant.

"Hey Gretchen, I feel like I'm spiraling out of control. My anxiety is at an eleven. It's likely I'm not going to be able to take on any new project any time soon. I will be out of commission until further notice. I am having a mental health crisis right now."

Von So-and-So assimilated this information quickly and responded to this email right away. "Let me know what I can do to help and no worries. I will contact each client personally to let them know that you will not be taking on any further freelance work at this time but that you may be open to collaborating with them at some point in the future."

Jill approved of the way that Von So-and-So handled her business by always remaining professional and by leaving the doors for communication open. She liked the way that her assistant's response gave her the space to recover from her depression in her own time and at her own pace. A luxury that she never could have afforded herself before in her life.

DING DONG

Jill received another email from Von So-and-So as soon as the German national landed back in the States from her winter ski trip to the Alps.

"I will be popping over in the next few days, with good news and to check in on you!" The message read.

Jill's mood gradually lifted as she began looking forward to finally receiving good news. In fact, she even managed to pick up the phone and call Persephone to reschedule follow-up therapy with her after she canceled her appointment the day prior because she felt like shit.

In her next session, she wanted to tell Persephone how she had planned to stop drinking soon in favor of creating a strong support network of women, her chosen family, that could support her sobriety and help her accept herself for who she was and help her figure out how to manage her mental illness and juggle the things in her professional life and personal life all at the same time.

Jill was still dead set on not drinking when Von So-and-So showed up on her doorstep the next day, dangling a bottle of very expensive champagne in her face. Attached to the bottle was a letter, in a plastic sleeve, it indicated that Jill had officially become a new business owner and a registered LLC.

Jill was carefully selecting the words that she was going to use to explain to Von So-and-So why she had stopped drinking, cold turkey, when Von So-and-So bent over, grabbed a cigarette out of Jill's pack and popped it in her mouth, as she continued to speak out of the side of her mouth.

"Oh wow, I did not know you were a smoker!" Jill said, scrambling to find a flame to light her assistant's cigarette with. You seem so health-conscious and all and you never smell like smoke. I think we may have more in common than I initially thought." Jill said in her attempt to bond with the anxious young woman.

"Jill, everyone has a right to keep their life private. There are many things you will never know about me. And I do not smell because my shit does not stink," Von So-and-So said rather matter of factually. "I am satisfied that everything's coming up roses for us now. Do you happen to have a flute?" She inquired.

"No, but I did play the French Horn in high school."

"Stupid American!" Von So-and-So muttered under her breath as she grabbed that expensive bottle of champagne by the throttle, ripped the foil off the cork with her teeth, propped one Bavarian sock up on the windowsill, with her Birkenstocks peeking out as she screwed the pop top off in the crease of her skirt, and drank the bubbles straight out of the bottle.

"Well, that's one way to celebrate!" Jill responded.

"This just means more bubbles for me, is all!" Von So-and-So continued to drink from the bottle before wiping the liquid sticky off her wet mouth with the thick of her wool-darned sweater.

"Sexy!" Jill stated sarcastically as she crossed her arms over her chest.

"Oh, cut me some slack!" Von So-and-So snapped back. "I just spent an entire week with my family on a ski trip from hell, and they are brutally honest people, you know."

"You don't say!" Jill said as Von So and So polished off the rest of the bottle "So, what have you been doing all this time I was gone? Writing?"

"Oh nuthin' Jill said as she lay across her lover's bed eating Ding Dongs for breakfast,"

"Sounds about right," Von So-and-So said as she handed Jill the empty bottle insisting that she place it in the recycle bin.

A VISION IN WHITE

With a sigh, Jill tried to make herself comfortable in the dusty, raggedy-ass old chair in Persephone's office but the truth is that she felt like she was stuck in therapy.

"I mean, I guess I thought I was aging gracefully until these hot flashes kicked into maximum overdrive. And I really started to feel like I was either going to get my ass kicked or I was going to kick the living shit out of somebody else and just some total random stranger, on the street, walking by, who happened to snap off or look at me sideways, or who tried to ask me for directions or who gave me shitty looks because I was jamming out to my favorite tunes—or just whoever I saw that pissed me off first, I guess.

I just wanted to haul off on somebody and really hit them with my best shot, you know? And then it got so bad, at one point, that I even found myself aggressively brushing shoulders with tourists who had accidentally found themselves walking down the wrong side of the street outside.

Maybe they had their head buried in their cell phones, searching for directions, because they were lost, and they happened to drift off course, without paying attention to the unwritten rules of this place.

Maybe they found themselves on the wrong side of the street, where I was walking, at breakneck speed, to avoid encountering anyone, and I refused to get out of their way so I would brush shoulders with them aggressively, as if they were supposed to know which side of the street to walk on in the first place, even though they were technically out of towners.

I mean, I was totally flying off the handle left and right. Or, how about this other example. Take all those times when I found myself raging at these asshole losers who do not understand that there is such a thing as elevator etiquette, meaning that you should always let the rider step off an elevator before you step on.

So I guess the real moral to this story, for me doc, is that booze and hot flashes are a recipe for total disaster! Wouldn't you agree?"

"Excuse me, could you repeat that? I wasn't listening." Persephone confessed.

"Oh never mind, what is the use of explaining any of this shit to anyone anymore. I mean, the last healthcare professional I spoke to literally tried to shove that behavioral therapy shit down my throat when I was in the throes of an internal three-alarm fire."

"And how did THAT make you feel?" The therapist asked.

"Are you kidding me? What a stupid question." Jill rolled her eyes as she chewed on a piece of bubble gum.

"Let me ask you something, Jill. How do you picture your own happily ever after? And by that I mean, what do you want your future to look like?"

"Well, gee whiz, I hadn't thought of it. Nobody ever asked me an important question like that before really." Jill found herself stumped as she leaned into the conversation with a renewed interest in figuring herself out.

"I think it is high time you became more future-focused, if you know what I mean by that." Persephone stated. "And the reason for this is because life is but a dream with a never ending current that is pulling you in one direction or another. and the only thing that is certain is our death!" She dramatically lifted her body up, elevating herself as she moved away from her

Herman Miller chair as if there had been a possession and some invisible entity was controlling her exaggerated movements, like a puppet, as she stepped up in front of a large easel which had an oversized sketch pad propped up on it.

"Behold, A vision in white!" She proclaimed as she presented the blank canvas, in front of her, with a grand sweeping motion of her sharp claws. Do you understand why I am referring to this page in that way?" She inquired.

"No."

"Simple!" Because I want you to understand that not every vision in white is about a wedding." Persephone continued to speak in a slow and measured tone, using her professional voice. "You really haven't got a clue, or have you?"

"I'm sorry." Jill stated. "I was daydreaming."

"Anyways, back to my story." Persephone insisted. "A true vision in white is like a blank canvas that only you can create.

It is far beyond the pale of that white wedding dress that is slowly receding into your rear view mirror. What is beyond the pale of that white wedding dress for you? What is your true purpose on earth? Who has shown up for you? Do they deserve a place on your vision board? A place in the sun? Who is going to be lucky enough to share the rest of your life journey with you? After all, you are already halfway there and living on a prayer."

"Please, don't remind me."

"What are all those *Needless Things*, as Stephen King put it, those pesky things that go bump in the night that you could do without because you have learned a priceless lesson. What are they? Who are they? Why are you still holding on to relics from the past?" She kept hammering Jill with questions until the patient could no longer take it anymore and she cried out.

"STOP IT!" Jill screamed at the top of her lungs as she covered her ears like the monkey on the basket in the lobby to protect herself from hearing the truth but Persephone was relentless in her pursuit of it.

"Let me demonstrate for you, the very genius of my own wild imagination as I create my very own vision board right in front of your eyes!" Persephone picked up a can of blood-red paint and hurled it at her vision board spontaneously, like Jill had imagined Jackson Pollock might.

The result was wild and frenetic to the core which made Jill flinch as she held her hand to her face to look away from that monstrosity of a masterpiece called art as if it were a total eclipse of the sun
.

While the paint was still wet and dripping down off the white page, Persephone introduced Jill to a wild cast of characters that she had created by cutting silhouettes out of a magazine. She would us them as paper dolls in her chaotic world of total make believe.

QUITE CONTRARY

"Well, hellooo G.G., if that IS, in fact, still your pseudonym!" Mary cackled, like a witch, at the cadence of her own witty remark.

Typical of someone with narcissistic tendencies,

Shivers of rage ran up and down Jill's spine. She closed her eyes and told herself to breathe deeply, as she knew her hormones must be in flux and totally out of wack but then she lost her shit all together and totally lashed out at Mary.

"No MARY! It is just Jill, this time, okay? And I am returning YOUR insane number of calls, as a courtesy TO YOU, so please do not act like you are the one who is doing me a favor by accepting this return call because I want you to know that I have got your number! You are always trying to guilt trip me about something, especially when it comes to making art. Well, not anymore!"Jill went off on Mary because she preferred to end their conversation sooner rather than later.

"Well then, how come you never call me anymore?" Mary made a valid point but Jill was in no mood to talk to Mary.

Meanwhile, Mary kept carrying on, the way she always had, bragging about some random bloke she met, in some exotic place, that none of her friends had ever met in real life.

AND that is because bottom feeders don't make house calls. They can't afford the gas money to rise to the top.

"I left you dozens of messages last week alone, and the week before." Mary continued to bitch and moan.

"I have been unwell, OKAY!"

"Well, anyways, I wanted to have dinner when I came to visit Chicago so that I could introduce you to Enrique."

"Enrique? Who the hell is that? No, forget I asked. You know what Mary? NEVER-MIND. Really, I never want to know. Please keep those scam stories confidential, and I mean it! I don't want to be part of your schoolgirl mentality crushes anymore, I need real friends who actually know how to act like grownups!

"And, for your information, I got depressed around the holidays and I just managed to pull my ass out of a major funk. So give me a break Mary!"

"Jill, everyone gets depressed from time to time. You know, when I get depressed I like to run a hot bath and pour in a generous amount of my favorite bath oil filled with bubbles, bath bombs and body lotion is where it's at!"

Jill knew that no matter what her neurotypical friends had to say about bubble-baths, breathing easy, or any other half ass solution she had cooked up to use as a band-aid to be slapped on her bleeding heart to conceal the true nature of her mental condition twas simply no lasting solution for because suicide still existed so basically Mary was totally full of shit in her eyes.

Jill was the one who could see the truth at the end of the dark tunnel. The one she had desperately tried to claw her way out of poverty and depression, knuckle over bloody fist while Mary was still clinging to her daydreams of romance in order to find salvation.

"Oh, Uhu." Jill flipped Mary the bird from the other side of the screen they were speaking on. "So, that is really your advice Mary? Just take a fucking bubble bath? Just take a fucking bath and rub the lotion all over my skin, really?"

"Well, I know it works magic for me, every time. I just take a good soak and think about all the wonderful things that I have to look forward to in life." She then suggested that Jill use the GLAD technique. "Do you know what that is?"

Mary was asking a question that Jill refused to answer.

"Mary, you DO NOT suffer from a diagnosed mental illness so why the fuck are you trying to give someone who actually does struggle, like me, any sort self help advice about depression when you really don't know shit about the way our minds works?" Jill went off on Mary again. "Why are you running your mouth?"

"What about all the voicemail messages that I left you the other week to tell you that I was coming to Chicago soon?"

"What about them?" Jill snapped.

"Well, I really wanted to hang out with you? You should know that isolating only makes your condition significantly worse, since you are the depressed person."

"Oh, is THAT a fact, *Mary*?" Jill snapped back. "And why is that?" She smacked her lips together as she stood in her lover's kitchen, hovering over the refrigerator, with her arm dangling over the door. She was savagely searching for leftovers to reheat, when standing there began to remind her of that image of the monster that she had seen the other day in her therapist office.

Jill took this vision as a sign from God who was sending her signals to beware of the monsters in her life because she knew she needed to start weeding her garden and the devil must be the first to go.

Her stomach was growling hard core. This was a sure fire sign that she was about to scarf down a million calories worth of holiday leftovers, in one afternoon, all in an effort to fill the spatial void she was feeling inside.

"I had to break things off with Roman over the holidays." Mary confessed before she began to sob.

"Oh, no kidding?" Jill rolled her eyes. "What happened?"

"Well, whatever happened, that is all water under the bridge now." Mary began to release the longest sigh that Jill had ever heard. "Maybe I should give up on love."

"Maybe you should focus on something more attainable, like making art." Jill reminded Mary, "like trying to complete that sequel to *Taken By Storm*."

"Oh, I couldn't possibly complete that project because I am weary and heartbroken and I can't write like that." Mary began to rationalize all the reasons why she felt that she was failing to complete her life's work which Jill did not want to hear.

"But you must finish it! I implore you!" Jill insisted, with all the might she could muster. "You never finished telling their story! I have to know if they will end up together." She insisted.

"I think you already know, Jill."

"I do?" Jill was flabbergasted.

"Maybe you can pick up the story where hey left off and choose your own adventure," Mary suggested.

"I feel cheated and confused." Jill confessed.

"Maybe you feel cheated and confused in another ways." Mary dropped a truth bomb that Jill did not want to hear. "I cannot write your future for you Jill. We leave those things to GOD."

"But wait! You failed at your mission in life Mary, to be a great writer. I just want you to know that I only returned your call as a courtesy, FY fucking I." Jill said, to drive home her hatred.

What the fuck do you want from me, for real? Do you want me to say that I will take on more clients for you so you can burn more bridges, and waste even more time and miss greater opportunities talking to scammers who DM you on IG instead of spending this precious time, that you have left, feeding your head, which is what artists should fucking do? Don't you remember that song, sis? Jefferson Airplane warned us a very long time ago about feeding your head so it's time to weed your garden."

"Well that certainly is one perspective."

"No Mary, it is the only perspective. Yoda says "There is no try."

"True."

"Art is a lifestyle that you must actively participate in, period. Everything else is imitation, artificial intelligence, and pure hyperbole. We must continue to dig deep. These connections that you claim to have with these random strangers you meet online are strictly superficial because they will be forgotten but great books are passed down from generation to generation.

You only have your own LIFE to waste Mary and that clock is ticking. I think you may be too far from the forest to see the trees anymore. You are afraid of elevating yourself. Afraid of great heights but your spirit has flown away, adrift aimlessly, as it hovers helplessly, left to witness everything from above the clouds, as a watcher but never a participant. You need to find a way to go in for the kill.

You have neglected your children for the sake of worshiping false kings that do not exist because you made them up...Are you aware of this? You treat your kids as if they are only an extension of your love for someone new.

I will have you know that I despise that level of mothering because it is so neglectful. I find it criminal, narcissistic and totally fucking vain. As a matter of fact, I find it tantamount to child abuse, due to neglect, because that is how they will see it in the end, that you always put a stranger's love for you before their own. Is that the way you want to be remembered? Is it?"

"You know, my grade school principal always said, during the morning announcements 'If you don't have anything nice to say about someone, don't say anything at all!'"

"Oh, Jesus Mary! I don't give a flying fuck what your school principal said, that experience is in the past." She clapped back in a mocking way.

"School has been out of session for you for a long time, Mary, just like you were a writer once, only now that experience has faded into the rear view mirror with all your other wins.

You are like a broken record and who the fuck wants to keep repeating the same mistakes they made yesterday over and over again until they are repeating the same song and dance!"

"Oh, so now we are going to start throwing around insults and get all highfalutin and fancy with this bickering match. You see how you are? I mean, really! You are so stuck up! So, tell me, what have you been doing with your time lately?" Mary asked, "Because I do have a few new clients I could send your way but you have to promise not to screw things up again!"

"Well, if you really must know AND since you asked," Jill said, "I have been super busy ghostwriting for my own clients. In addition, I have been on a painful path of self discovery. "And furthermore," she added. "I will have you know that you are currently looking at the new owner of an incorporated LLC! That's right, I am the proud female owner of my own business!" Jill held a document up to the screen.

SHOW AND TELL

Jill found herself sitting on that dusty, raggedy-ass old chair again, with that monster from the cannibal portrait leering at her with lascivious eyes, as she waited for her therapist to call her back to the dungeon for therapy.

This time you bit off more than you can chew and now I hope you choke to death on all those sharp bones you swallowed whole, you creepy son of a bitch!

Jill lashed out at the monster in her head, as she eyeballed the unsettling masterpiece. Next, she turned her attention to that googly-eyed monkey trash can that was seated at the foot of the gory masterpiece.

a*nd how exactly did you manage to escape from my invisible purse? You spooky ass yellow eyed little bitch! Be gone!*

She squeezed her eyes closed tight to wish the monkey away, when all of a sudden, her mind was flooded with memories she did not want to have, like relics from her past.

She was experiencing a flashback from decades ago. A throwback to one of the most painful experiences she could remember, back to a time when her mother used to make her sit on a chair in timeout as punishment for stretching the truth and telling lies.

It was during these lonely times, that she learned to create make believe worlds in my mind. Her Mother would often just leave her sitting there, on that chair, for hours, watching life unfold around her while she was off gallivanted around town walking the dog while chatting up the neighbors, socializing with friends, shopping for the latest fashions or simply enjoying an afternoon cocktail at the corner pub before taking off to go cruising with the flavor of the week while her daughter just sat on that chair.

Jill had spent so much of her time alone, feeling punished for silly things or innocent mistakes. But, in her solitude she managed to develop a very keen powers of observation and that is when she became a young visionary.

No sooner had Jill's mind started to assimilate all of these fantastical big-picture ideas when suddenly Persephone appeared, as if from out of nowhere, rising from the pitch black darkness as if she was standing in the midst of a slow-moving city fog machine that billowed out smoke which curled up around the hem of her slow-moving hooped skirt, dissipating into the folds of the frock as the dress dusted the floor to and fro like that animated broom from the movie Fantasia, sweeping the area with broad and dancing gestures.

Persephone was cinched into a crimson-and-coal colored, crushed velvet steampunk gown pulled so tight that she reminded Jill of an upright insect moving in strangely divided sections as she led her client into the darkness of night like some bizarre insect straight out of a Hieronymus Bosch hellscape.

She looks like some sort of gothic black widow in that crazy ass period piece.

Jill rubbed her eyes raw and turned her head sideways to study the details of that costume as Persephone took a seat underneath the artificial light above her desk to begin the session.

Persephone was seated, posture perfect, at her old school typewriter, wearing her neat pill hat while recording the details of Jill's mental health journey in her own words, as if she were penning her unauthorized biography.

Persephone is phony." Jill was considering the possibilities of this being true as Persephone cracked her knuckles over her typewriter as a warm-up before she began pounding away on it. She popped up out of her chair and drifted across the room, to that crimson landscape she had created at their last session, by splashing paint on a blank page. "Get ready. I'm about to introduce some new characters to my vision!" She announced.

"But first, I want to share something I just discovered about myself." Jill said. "My mother never believed anything I ever told her and now I write fiction for a living."

When Persephone had no response to her ironic insight, this is when Jill began to feel like sessions were really all about what Persephone had to say and not about her. Jill was starting to get the impression that Persephone's presentation had been performed many times before, and not for the sake of her audience.

Jill felt left out of the healing process that she was supposed to be experiencing and so she began to feel hot under the collar and have a hot flash, which was making it very uncomfortable for her to sit still for much longer listening to this self-aggrandizing garbage.

She was getting ready to blow her stack when she finally opened up her mouth to say, "When is it my turn for show and tell? Our time is almost up!"

"Excuse me?" Persephone retaliated by lashing out. "Do not control the progress of this session!" She insisted. "I am the expert here and I was in the middle of telling a story," Persephone said, "a story which is as significant to me as it will be to you. It teaches a valuable life lesson and one that you desperately need to learn."

"Well, I am a pretty quick study and I think I already learned my lesson! It's called don't pay a narcissist to tell you their story when they will gladly share it with you for free! And now, if you will excuse me, I will be leaving to focus on my own visions of the future WITHOUT your unsolicited input! I have learned everything I need to know about AND, If I happen to have an outstanding unpaid invoice OR you think that I owe you anything, which I highly fucking doubt, you can contact my assistant Von So-and-So, otherwise, your own time is up!"

"Who?" Persephone asked.

"You know, Von So-and-So, my personal assistant! Jesus Christ, You haven't heard a damn word I say or am I just another sick cash cow to you?" Jill stormed out of therapy.

On the way home she stopped into Walgreens to purchase an oversized piece of white cardboard to create her own vision board on.

I don't need some crazy stupid bitch to tell me how to make art!

After that she stopped at the ATM to pull some money out when she happened to glance down at the balance on her receipt which made her feel like she had just won the lottery because she had never seen so many zeros before in all of her life!!! She dropped everything she was doing at once in order to call Von So-and-So for an explanation.

Von So-and-So was so excited as she explained to Jill, in detail, how every single one of the account's receivable invoices came back paid immediately and the money was transferred.

MAD MAX

Just as Jill was about to gain some real steam in her life—just before she really started to feel like she was control of her own destiny again, right around the holidays, after she spent so many agonizing hours isolated and completely alone, thrashing around in pools of her own sweat and tears as she listened to the sound of sirens fill the night sky —that is when Max decided to give Jill a call.

Hearing the sound of his deep, dark, Darth Vader-esque voice soothed her aching soul. Those calls meant everything to her because their bond was pure fire. Max told Jill that he was going to be in town for business next month and he wanted to take her to dinner then.

"Flying back to Manhattan first thing the next morning but I thought you might like to get together. You pick the restaurant and I will make the reservation, anyplace you want." He added. "I can get us in, absolutely." He really poured on the charm.

Jill squealed with delight at the sound of this exciting news. She was jumping up and down, clapping her hands together, like a schoolgirl with a crush, which sent her giant boobs flopping around, spinning in opposite directions.

VIVID VOID

The following morning Jill rose from her lover's bed, bright eyed and all bushy tailed in order to work on own vision board. She lit a cigarette and stood in front of the vivid void for a very long time. Her vision board stood in stark contrast to the exquisite and ornate collectibles that surrounded her in real life.

All the precious things he left behind. All forgotten and collecting dust. Does he only take me out of the box when he wants to play with me?

Jill rolled the pad of her index finger along the dusty edge of one of his most treasured relics as she began to have doubts about their future together. She was experiencing a longing for him that was so acutely that she was having sharp pains in her chest because she had struggled to hold on their future for so long.

Love is not ownership.

Jill reminded herself as her heart sank. Max had never introduced her to his family or many of his friends but somehow he still managed to stay in touch with her after all those years.

Jill could not accept the fact that she desired being a kept woman and that gifts had become her love language. Jill had fantasized about being subservient to a powerful alpha male ever since Max threw a hundred dollar bill down on his dresser and told her to grab a cab home after they fucked like maniacs on their first date together many moons ago.

Jill refocused her attention on how Max had just asked her out for dinner because she so desperately needed his love to look forward to in life.

"Sure, take me to dinner." Jill flirted shamelessly with Max, "Just don't bring that stormy weather to the Midwest." She always tried to say something clever , in a sexy way, to keep his interest.

THE FUTURE WILL BE

The next few weeks were a complete and utter haze of smoke filled with spells of euphoria as Jill rowed her boat gently down the stream of life, surrendering to her daydreams and flights of fancy, as she crash dieted and roamed aimlessly around the city
remembering all the places she wanted to go again with her lover.

Jill had waited, for so long, for this vision of the future to include Max and she wanted it to be an expression of the deep and meaningful connection they had since they had known each other for so long. Jill hoped that she was going to be around for this future with Max that would be filled with sunshine and luxury cruises, long after his other lovers disappeared in a boating accident.

Jill fired up her one-hitter and took a major drag as she languished in her own hysterical laughter. She was beyond high as she feverishly flipped through the stacks of the travel and leisure magazines that she had surrounded herself with as he eyes darted quickly back and forth across the glossy pages.

Stacks of these lifestyle magazines were beginning to pile up in the kitchen, in the bedroom, and in the bathroom on the floor beside the toilet.

She had cut people out of them, and they were lying like paper dolls that were ready to dress, spread out all over the floor. Some of them served as models of her as she was dressing them in exactly the kind of fashion that she imagined herself wearing when she took the throne beside her king.

She was cutting out a silhouette of Max that she intended to paste in the center of her vision board – because Max was the center of her universe – when all of a sudden Von So-and-So stormed through the front door.

PICTURE OF YOU

"Well, entrez s'il vous plait," Jill joked as her assistant began dipping her tea bag anxiously into the boiling water that she just poured into her thermos cap.

"Jill," Von So-and-So said, dipping her bag in her tea way too many times to count in a restless up and down motion.

"Yeeesssss," Jill drew out her response because she was in a happy and playful mood.

"Jill, you are way, WAY behind on your deadlines. Do you care to share what is going on here? I mean, what is all this crap?" Von So-and-So said as she maneuvered around the piles of magazines, that Jill had stacked, as if Von So-and-So were navigating a maze, in order to find a place where she could sit down.

"Well, for your info, I have been working on a vision of my future." Jill proudly announced to her house guest. "Per the insistence of my therapist, of course. She said it was an important part of my journey so I must complete it."

"Oh really? Is that a fact!" Von So-and-So broke out into laughter but strangely did not seem the least bit amused.

"Yes, really!" Jill said in a braggart sort of way as she folded her arms over her chest like a champ. "Take a look-see!"

"What is the purpose of this preposterous mess?" Von So-and-So blurted out bluntly. "We can't sell this garbage. It is worse than a high school art project." She let out a long sigh of discontentment, as she stood up and rushed to the kitchen.

Von So-and-So stopped at the sink, dropped her whole hand

into that boiling hot cup of tea, yanked out the herbal tea bag, rang the hot water out of it with her bare hand and then pitched the bag into the sink. "For later, in case you want tea. You can recycle that bag. Beggars can't be choosers you know," she said as her hand shook in anger. "I use them at least twice."

"Good to know." Jill replied. "Tough crowd!" She rolled her eyes to heaven as she followed Von So-and-So out of the kitchen to return to the same space where they had been sitting in front of her vision of the future.

Jill began to drone on about how that vision board was about her future with Max because it represented how her life would unfold, when Von So-and-So finally stopped Jill cold turkey to ask, "Who the hell is Max? I have never met this man."

Jill was trying to explain who Max was but Von So-and-So did not care. In fact, she finally stopped Jill, mid-explanation. "He is nothing but a distraction for you now. We have moved past the point of trivial distractions." She continued to lay into her boss and really tell it like it is. "You know, if you complete the list of jobs I compiled for you, you can afford to buy the condominium you are currently standing in, from Max without ever bothering to see his face ever again. If he loved you he would have been here for you. You need to get a real life."

To put a finer point on it, Von So-and-So handed Jill a very professional-looking file folder that contained a colorful PowerPoint presentation, that she had created and then printed out in order to demonstrate the precise steps that Jill needed to take, including a legally binding contracts that Max would need to sign in sell his place to her. They were all color coded in Appendix A of that file folder.

"Get a good price for it and then run." Von So-and-So said.

"And, you need to start writing again soon if you want to put this plan to buy his condo into action when he finally materializes here in real life.

"Think about it!" Von So-and-So said. "What do you really want out of this connection you have, Jill? Your life is already halfway over and the cavalry is not coming for you, so you must step up to the plate and reach for the stars while you are still so high up on that ladder in life and I am telling you that home ownership is where your fortune begins!"

And with that, Von So-and-So turned around and left, slamming the door behind her on the way out, causing a chain reaction that made the drying glue on the back of Max's paper doll, from Jill's vision board, detach itself and glide down to the floor, where it landed like a dead body in the middle of a crime scene, with his twisted arm around his broken neck.

DIFFICULT

Max spotted Jill at the bar and eagerly approached her, all smiles, greeting her as if he had just seen her yesterday, wearing her favorite *Acqua Di Gio* cologne.

They were so familiar with each other, after so many years, that no words need to be spoken between them for Jill to feel the love that they had for each other, the energy that vibrated between them when they hovered in each other's orbit was pure magic and she knew that he knew what she was thinking about. She simply felt that they belonged together because it was their destiny. They fit together like the pieces of a complex puzzle. Later that night she planned to submit and make love to him at The Drake hotel.

Jill knew that she may have Max as her captive audience for only one night and one night only. She also knew that, after they made love, she would soon feel empty again inside.

She wanted to be closer to Max. She wanted him to reveal to her more than he ever had before about himself. She had actually spent hours and days thinking about what questions she might ask him once she got the chance.

How do you take your coffee?

She decided that she needed to know the answer to that questions that she wondered about for a very long time. These were the sort of details, about a lover, that Jill thought another lover oughta know.

Jill was so horny that she could feel it in her loins as her pussy buzzed with excitement as if to say FEED ME and he was thirsty too.

She could feel her pussy pulsating against his inner thigh after he took off his pants. Still, she wondered where else his cock had been as she grabbed the shaft in her hand and began to tug on it, pumping it hard and up and down in the palm of her hand.

She asked him about other women. He did not respond other than to compliment her for a hand-job well done. He only gave her the vaguest of clues that he may be in a serious relationship with someone else but Jill knew not to ask too many questions because she did not want to appear difficult.

"How do you take your coffee?" She jerked him off a little slower.

"Really?" He exhaled as she laughed. "Why do you want to know this now?" He raised one eyebrow to look down at her. "Okay," he finally said, "I take it black."

"I never got to have breakfast with you." Jill confessed.

"Is it her?" She asked delicately.

"Is it her?" He repeated the question in order to give himself time to think of an answer.

"HER…HER, that hottie you met at Hooters around the same time you met me? That woman who modeled for Maxim? You know what, Max? Never mind because I really do not care who you are with anymore. You have wasted so much of my life not choosing me. This really sucks!"

"Sucks!" Max repeats the word before he says "I like the sound of that word."

"Are you aware that we have only been together for a grand total of six months, over the past two decades, but I have been in love with you the whole time?

Anyways, none of that matters anymore. The reason why I

wanted to meet with you today was to tell you that I want to buy your condo because I need a place that I can call home and I already picked out the curtains. And besides, you told me that you were trying to sell it. Will you sell it to me for a good price?"

Max laughed in Jill's face. "Yeah, right. I'll make you an offer you can't refuse? You must be joking. You know sometimes I think that you think that money just grows on trees Jill. What are you talking about?

I am the one who pays ALL your bills. I am the one that keeps you fed, with a roof over your head. I am the one who pays for you. You needed me to survive this pandemic when you were swimming in debt and had no place left to live because your life was falling apart. What would have you done without me? You were so helpless. You had no one and nothing. You were freaking out!"

"Since you 'rescued me' from my hell-on-earth Ohio experience, I have been bending over backward to make you fall in love with me all over again and this means nothing to you!

It is clear now that you just want to have your cake and eat other people's pussy too and that is not the way this relationship is going to play out because I am getting ready to take control of my own life and choose my own fucking adventure!"

"Look, I am feeling kind of attacked here. I mean, do you want to have sex or not?" Max threw his hands in the air before he yanked up his jeans. "I think I lost my hard on."

"So did I!" Jill stood in front of him with her arms crossed over her chest.

"Why are you being so difficult?" Max asked. You are not as fun as you used to be. This use to be so uncomplicated, this thing we had."

"I am not in the business of not being complicated anymore.

That ship has sailed." She stated. "I want to buy your condo." She approached him as he parked his ass on the hotel bed to review the paperwork she dropped in his lap.

"I want a forever home, in the city, and I think it might be yours." She said, handing him the financial records that proved that she had more than enough money in the bank to cover all the expenses.

"I trust that all my assets are in place," Jill said as she bent over to slowly pick up the pen that she had dropped on the floor in front of him.

WHERE THE HEART IS

It felt really great to have a safe landing after Jill just experienced losing the love of her life, and forever, but by choice.

She invited Shantay over as soon as she could pull herself together long enough for them to celebrate. They spent the day lounging in her brand new matching blue Cubs stadium chairs, binge-eating ice cream and wolfing down pizza while Jill showed Shantay all the new comedy reels that she had written material for.

Shantay was scrolling and selecting a few of the videos to watch. In one of them the performer said: "Chicago is the kind of city where people stop to take photos of themselves flipping the bird to Trump tower from the Lasalle street bridge and for the longest time I thought they were telling me to fuck off, so that was one crazy experience I had."

"Oh damn! That is so true. I have seen them do that!" Shantay giggled with glee as she kicked her feet out in front of her like she was propelling a paddle boat. "You are for sure going to be laughing all the way to the bank with cracks like this Jill."

"Facts I try to keep my shit one hundred!" Jill agreed.

"So, when are you going to throw this better than the black and white ball housewarming party you've been talking about?" Shantay hinted because she wanted the first invite.

"You will be the first to know." Jill confessed, "But this will not be a catered affair. Instead it will be an elegant dinner party because I want to showcase the many new culinary skills that I perfected during lock-down, and... AND!" Jill started to get really excited.

"I plan to make this 'Windy City Women' party an annual event, and you will be there of course! Sitting right next to me, at the head of my decked-out dining room table, as my guest of honor, along with Von So and So. "And we shall usher forth a new renaissance filled with fashion and art!"

* * *

Jill spent a long time in her new home happily puttering around alone as she worked on clearing her head and blessing the place with sage before she hung curtains.

It was a cold day but she was sitting in one of those blue stadium chairs, in HER new condo, with a joint in one hand, and a glass of pink Champagne in the other, with all the windows wide open because her ex-lover was still paying the electric bill and she wanted to watch her new curtains sway in the wind as she listened to her favorite music in a place she called home. It felt so electrifying to feel the city roaring back to life after so many lonely years spent alone, listening to the sound of the sirens.

Jill took a second look at that vision board that Max was no longer a part of and that made her smile. She wondered if Max thought that he had dodged a bullet by losing her the other woman. Jill had always considered herself damaged goods ever since the day she was diagnosed with a mental illness which made her feel less than desirable. Jill was painfully aware of her own limitations because she had experienced a failure to launch so many times in her miserable life.

She knew she could not hold down a 9 to 5 job. She knew that she could not shower and dress herself consistently at the same time each morning. She knew she was a neurotic hypochondriac because she was afraid of heights, spiders, snakes, and the list just kept going on and on in her mind until she began to obsess over all these things that she was obsessing about.

She managed to pull herself together for long enough to send a cryptic group text to her business partners. It simply said "I cannot write because my heart is broken."

Von So-and-So responded immediately, "I am so sorry this has happened to you. I will respond to your clients, on your behalf, until you are able to start writing again if that is okay with you."

The next text message came from Shantay and it said, "We got you girl, we know the drill. Hang in there! We are here to help! I know there are to be no guests on your visitation list, including Max, and your groceries will be delivered directly to your suite, first thing every week, until further notice. I know this hurts like hell, Jill, but I am convinced that you did the right thing and I think you are really brave!"

"You do? Cool! Now I am going to change the locks, change my phone number, and cry my eyes out." Jill confessed.

"Excellent idea!" You made the right choice by cutting him out. It was the right thing to do, Jill. You will heal, give it time.

He is likely living a double life anyways, and trash is trash, at least. I mean, hell, who knows how many lies he is living and who cares? I am just thankful that whatever he does from now on is not going to concern you anymore because you are on a clear trajectory straight to the top WITHOUT this man!"

Jill removed Italy from her vision board because it had been her life long dream to travel there, on her honeymoon, with Max on her arm. Then she tossed out all the images that reminded her of him including his preference for certain types of women like Sasha Tara.

And, since it was Valentine's Day when she destroyed her vision board, she decided she was going to treat herself to chocolate and cappuccino laced lunch so she took a stroll over to

Fannie May, on the opposite side of the river, near the loop while everyone flipped Trump Tower the bird.

I HAVE THE POWER

Not long after parting ways with Max and spending yet another Valentine's Day alone, Jill finally snapped out of her funk to find herself three pounds heavier but no worse for the wear, and with her life and career still fully intact, ready and waiting for her to return to the life she loved.

She was amazed by how she was able to simply snap back after suffering a major blow, to her heart like that, followed by a long spell of sadness but once she did start writing again, Jill noticed that something had fundamentally changed about the way she viewed comedy, as a middle aged woman, versus how she felt before she was over the hill.

In her youth Jill had preferred to remain anonymous and very much behind the scenes because she could not handle being criticized or heckled on stage by strangers but the older she was getting the less she seemed to give a damn what other people thought because she had basically stopped giving a shit altogether.

BANG BANG!

Jill was showing the new material she had written for other comedians to Shantay who was laughing her ass off as she watched the comedy reels roll by on her feed.

Shantay turned away from her cell phone, at one point, to say to Jill, "You know, you should be performing this material yourself. You are really funny and that way you could make more money than these clowns."

"You mean it?" Jill smiled broadly while still somewhat doubting the power of her own God-given talent.

"Oh, without a doubt. This shit is comedy gold. I am telling you. And, do you know what?" She smiled as she popped open a fresh bag of chips.

"What?" Jill listened enthusiastically.

"If you perform this show yourself I bet a bunch of women would come see you ranting and raving about all this miserable bullshit that women go through in life. You do know that misery loves company, right?"

"Perform my own comedy? I think that is a great idea." Jill smiled back. "In fact, I think I'll do just that!"

"You will? Well, you should!" Shantay got excited for her friend as she strategically nibbled on the corner of a chip.

"Just like that!" Jill, snapping her fingers and she made it happen.

ON WITH THE SHOW

Jill was getting ready to tackle performing live stand-up comedy for the first time in her life, when she slipped through the back door of a convention center that stood next to the venue where she should have been performing.

She was wandering around backstage, clueless, searching for a talent sign in sheet for open mic night, when this familiar face, a sweet senior, who reminded Jill a lot of

Betty White, popped her head out from behind an emerald curtain wearing a pair of white sequin jazz gloves as she motioned for Jill to take the stage.

"Well, come on sweetheart. They are all waiting for you! Is that what you are wearing?" Betty seemed disappointed.

"They are? Yes, this is what I am wearing, why?" Jill sounded puzzled as she blurted out "Wait, WHAT? I didn't even sign up for this!" She complained into the hot mic as she took center stage, in her checkered Converse high top sneakers, to perform her own comedy.

"Well, anyways, the show must go on!" Betty White said, flashing an expensive smile at Jill before she vanished into the wings.

"Well, I was hoping to start with some crowd work but considering that I can't see anyone." Jill squinted into the darkness that she perceived to be the audience. Suddenly the heat from the blinding spotlight above her head triggered a hot flash so fierce that she started tearing off her clothes.

"Maybe I'll get lucky and you will think this is all part of the act." She joked with the crowd. She was down to a wet bra with her jeans unbuttoned, at the fly, when she got a cat call from the audience which she took as an indication to start her stand up.

"What's so funny about depression?" She asked the audience

but nobody answered.

"I tend to get myself involved in crazy ass scenarios that neurotypical people would never find themselves caught dead in, that's what. I mean, you know, sometimes, it feels like I am living in a sitcom." She confessed.

"Take my dating life...please! If there was such a thing as a dating resume, mine would read, as a first bullet point, has a lot of experience in bed because she never gets out of it."

Jill waited for someone to laugh but nobody did.

A wise woman once told me I'd have more luck with men if I left the house once in a while so I tried that a few times and I end up dating a homeless guy that I met at a bar back in Ohio. You know the kind of dude that your friends try to warn you about but you don't pick up on anything they are putting down all because the dude is great in bed?

Well, this drifter swept me off my feet immediately by making all kinds of romantic types of gestures toward me. He even wrote me a poem once, on a napkin. He also picked me a bunch of wild flowers. Yeah. He picked them over at Peace cemetery on his way to meet me at this art gallery opening that he rode his bike to after he gave blood at the local bank.

One time I told him I did not want to have sex, because I didn't feel like it, and he had been camping out at my house, for over a week, so I asked him to leave, to give me some space, but he turned around and asks me if he could sleep in my car, because he had no place else to go that night so finally I put two and two together and discovered he was, in fact, homeless.

I recently had drinks, in the city, with some Southern gentleman. His profile was set on travel mode and his location was listed as O'hare Airport so, after I got done explaining to him that I was not a tourist ATM that he could make a deposit in and withdraw, during his layover, he turns around and says to me:

"Isn't your cat going to miss you if you don't get home soon?"

"What's so funny about depression?" Jill asked the audience

again and got crickets.

"Well, basically I've failed at every job I ever had. This is the kind of shit that happens when you cannot remain consistent with the routines you need to follow in life and you have zero control over your own emotions. So eventually I had to find the kind of job that I could not be fired from and that is when I stumbled over comedy. Because, as a comedian, you can wake up whenever the hell you want because there is no big boss man lording over your life anymore.

I never wanted a boss anyways. I never wanted to be a team player because I am basically only rooting for team ME now, ever since I turned 50.

Speaking of cats, some friend I once had, who was fully aware that I suffered from major depression for my whole life, mind you, once said to me, straight to my face, that I was allowed to be depressed, for like a week, if my cat died."

Suddenly some red-headed ginger in the audience started to laugh uncontrollably as he raised a paddle, with a number on it, straight up into the air for everyone to see.

Shamus McGillicuddy was his name and he had just placed a bid on Jill at a charity bachelorette auction that she did not know she was attending. And boy, did Shamus get his money's worth by taking Jill on a date because afterwards, when they got back to her house, she banged him like a bronco.

"Have you no shame, Shamus?" She repeated over and over again as she squealed out with delight all night.

THE HEADLINER

Von So-and-So placed Jill on a strict budget, from that day forth, because she had been blowing a lot of things including money lately, and explained to her that she needed to write more and focus on honing her craft, if she wanted to spend that kind of money and time on fashion and men.

Von So-and-So quickly devised a plan to help Jill earn more money by promoting her, as a comedian, through advertising and by helping her monetize her online content.

Shantay knew that Jill was a funny lady but she was doubled over laughing when she saw the raw footage from that stand-up show that she performed, by accident, in front of a bachelorette auction teaming with single studs.

"Von So-and-So is so right!" Shantay said, after she finally caught her breath to speak again, "You have got to post this on your social media platform because someone sent you a video of it and this mix-up is pure comedy gold. And the fact that you took it seriously and actually went on a date with this Shamus character makes this great story even more funny!"

After Jill went ahead and posted that mix-up on her social media accounts, she became an overnight sensation once again as she received hundreds of thousands of views and laughing emojis after she dropped the video.

The comments people left spoke volumes about how depression was rarely covered or discussed in mainstream media, let alone in such a social setting and by using such a public forum. People were thanking Jill for being so open and shockingly transparent about the struggles she faced with mental health and they were also thanking her for making her own personal experiences with these struggles so entertaining yet down right relatable. So many strangers, who had become her fans, reached out to tell her that they had felt so scared and alone before Jill exposed herself to the world by sharing her own true stories.

As a result of all this new attention, a whole bunch of fans started asking Jill if and when she might be performing next. Assuring her that if she did that they would certainly buy tickets for her show.

After Von So-and-So read through the comments on those latest reels, she approached Jill with another brilliant idea. "We should set up a GoFundMe page for you and for all of your fans to join since they said they would buy tickets to see you perform again live. And with that seed money," Von So-and-So said, "we can afford to host a charity event in order to bring awareness to these mental health issues that you care so much about."

Before long, Jill's GoFundMe had generated all the funds that her team needed to throw this lavish mental health awareness fundraiser, just like the one that Jill attended for Darling.

WHAT'S SO FUNNY ABOUT DEPRESSION?

Jill was thrilled that her charity event went off without a hitch, like a well orchestrated outdoor wedding on a perfect summer day, which seemed like a fitting metaphor for this new experience that would change her life forever after she decided to leave the love of her life in the rear view mirror and marry the career of her dreams.

The icing on that cake was that she had her two ride or die besties, Von So-and-So and Shantay, by her side, when this happened and to help her celebrate this amazing dream come true.

They had been there to support her through all of her trials and tribulations, ever since she moved back to the city. They were the ones who had played a pivotal role in launching her comedy career.

Jill had no idea if she was going to kill or bomb, on stage, at her very own charity event, but either way she was going to knock them dead and enjoy every moment of it because she had already raised a shit ton of money for a very good cause and she was determined to have a good time telling her story and she wanted to look great doing so. This is why she hired both Harlow and Cami to style her wardrobe for the event and Fang to make sure her nails were on point as Wheatley applied her makeup just right so that she could look dynamite for her special day.

Naturally, Jill had invited her friends, clients, and all the other artists she knew to be a part of it all but really it was Shantay who had made the greatest dent in ticket sales when she took it upon herself to invite a handful of wealthy philanthropists, who she was on a first name basis with, who lived in the various high dollar buildings where she use to worked, on the Gold Coast, where she mingled with millionaires.

The show was sold out and the venue was packed with wall to wall people with standing room only for the press and more foot traffic than Jill had seen, at any event, since before the pandemic.

"Well, this is probably the least most depressing day of my life thanks to all of you!" Jill praised her stylists prior to her performance. Then she tipped them triple the norm for services rendered before she stepped out on stage, to face an audience she could actually see for the first time in her life.

"Let us address the elephant in the room first, which is that having any kind of mental illness, including depression, is no picnic. I think we can all agree on that. It is really no laughing matter because. I mean, I could be homeless right now, and so could you, and that is the point.

Your neighbor could be homeless. The love of your life could be homeless. Take a look around because this could happen to anyone." She cautioned. "The point is, it could happen to anyone. It could be your turn to sleep under a bridge next and you never know…

As a matter of fact I think I dated a homeless man once so you can believe me when I tell you that people are not always into providing full disclosure, but nobody should live in fear or in shame. I think that is the bottom line for me. For me mental health awareness means specifically that every human is entitled to three hots and a cot, plain and simple.

Homelessness is rapidly reaching record numbers in America. And you mean to tell me that we are supposed to be the richest country on earth and we can't house our own? What a fucking joke!

I am so grateful that we could all come together here to support an amazing cause to house the homeless because everyone deserves a place they can call their home.

I prefer to cry before I laugh so I wanted to get that all out of the way before I started telling jokes." Jill confessed to a growing live audience who were now cheering and clapping for her.

"Allow me to introduce myself as I am new to the Chicago comedy scene. My name is G.G. Maxwell and I believe that every good story, which is basically what good comedy is all about, begins with a question like...What is so funny about depression?

Well, it makes you suffer from low self-esteem. I suffer from that low type of self esteem where I think about stupid shit while my mind is off to the races all day long thinking about stupid shit like...

Why doesn't he love me anymore? Is it because I have so many bad hair days? Why do some women in prison have better hair than I do?

Like, take for example that one chick, Lori whoever-the-hell Daybell, I mean come on! She's got that wind swept Daryl Hannah from *Mermaids* wind swept hair going on meanwhile, in another lock up facility, you have got Ruby the Ridiculous, the social media mommy mogul attending a hearing the other day and she's sporting some hair style that makes her look like she just stepped out of a Pantene shampoo commercial with waves for days. I mean come on! Here I am fifty years old, over the hill, and I still don't know how to properly use a fucking styling tool.

On the flip side though, you can take me to a cocktail party and I'm an instant hit because I drink like fish and I can't stick to one topic of conversation for more than five minutes at a time because everything and everybody bores me to tears and it's hard smiling your ass off the whole time, but before you know it...

I am on a first name basis with the smartest people in the room because I can tell a fascinating story for days and I know where all the best bathrooms are in the house because I've cased the joint looking for the backdoor.

I am a truly neurotic and I will be the first to admit that but I think that is mainly because I've been misdiagnosed so many times by now that the powers that be currently claim that I am suffering from every condition listed in the DSM5 and you know it's always easier to blame your problems and excuse your own bad behavior and poor life choices on something else so here we are.

But then I discovered weed so I thought everything was going to be hunky dory until I got fired from my job for smoking the only thing that ever made me get my ass out of bed and show up there in the first place.

But it's not really a big deal, I mean the part about being fired, that may be, considering that I have basically been fired from every job I ever had, until I took up comedy.

I tried my hand at substitute teaching for a minute but the kids ganged up on me and then sent me straight to the principal's office with a one word note that said DELUSIONAL.

I mean my resume is such a joke at this point that being a comedian is the only job I'm still qualified to keep and everyone knows that art is a gamble, and a super risky business, but then again, who has the last laugh now?"

Jill, the comedian, closed her show with a standing ovation and a crowd filled with fans who donated thousands of dollars to a worthy cause that was very close to her heart.

Made in United States
Troutdale, OR
04/25/2024